JUNK MALE

JUNK MALE

Colleen Tuohy

iUniverse, Inc.
Bloomington

JUNK MALE

This is a work of fiction. All of the characters, names, incidents, organizations, and dialogue in this novel are either the products of the author's imagination or are used fictitiously.

iUniverse books may be ordered through booksellers or by contacting:

iUniverse
1663 Liberty Drive
Bloomington, IN 47403
www.iuniverse.com
1-800-Authors (1-800-288-4677)

ISBN: 978-1-4502-9980-0 (sc)
ISBN: 978-1-4502-9981-7 (ebk)

Printed in the United States of America

iUniverse rev. date: 3/9/2011

ACKNOWLEDGEMENTS

I'd like to thank Ashley Sharman for his encouragement and guidance. Also, thank you Kelly Tuohy, my daughter, for always believing in me. Judy and Amy, thanks for the laughs.

Disclaimer and Introduction

The following stories are based on true events. The names and details have been changed to protect the guilty. If you think you recognize yourself, keep quiet. I won't tell who you are if you don't tell. Please be advised I'm Irish and as everyone knows, the Irish are famous for having the gift of gab. To save face (yours and mine), let's say the following stories are not true so in no way should anyone feel I am writing about them.

Junk Male is a humorous book of stories for both women and men to enjoy. Men will be able to say to their sweethearts, "Read this story. I'm not that bad after all." Single women will relate to their own unique experiences and married women will be able to judge if the grass is greener on the other side.

Contents

THE ACCOMPLICE

It was Friday night when Jasmine Walker called her best friend, Catherine. Jasmine was distraught because she thought her boyfriend of four years was cheating on her. This wasn't the first time she suspected him of cheating, but it was the first time she wanted to get proof.

His name was Ralph and he lived in a beautiful octagon shaped glass house he had built on top of a mountain, overlooking a lake. On one side of his house was a view of the lake, which was over a mile long and stocked with a variety of fish. There were many trumpet geese in and surrounding the water.

From the other side of the house was a view of the Blue Ridge Mountains. From each window in his house, the scenery rolled out in every direction. Every so often you could spot a reddish brown bushy tailed fox dashing by as it chased a rabbit or bird. Along with white-tailed deer, all of this nature made Ralph's land a wildlife watching opportunity.

Ralph had trees, plants and flowers of every kind brought in with markers in the ground stating the name and the region of each variety. Walking on his property was like visiting a museum of nature and he was always pleased to test your knowledge about trees, plants, flowers and wildlife. Of course he always knew the answers to the questions he would throw at you and was quick to point out if you were incorrect.

Once Jasmine had a girlfriend named Diane who was visiting her for a few weeks. One weekend, Jasmine drove Diane out to the country to see Ralph's beautiful refuge. Ralph bombarded Diane with a quiz about the different kinds of trees on his property. When Diane missed one of the questions, Ralph didn't hesitate to say, "Jasmine, I thought this was supposed to be one of your smart friends."

Ralph's property was about two hours from Jasmine's house and when they had plans together she would drive up and spend the weekend with him.

Ralph called Jasmine and told her he couldn't see her this weekend. He said he was leaving town so there was no need for her to drive up to see him. She said he mentioned it again before the conversation was over, which Jasmine thought was very odd. Not once had she ever driven up uninvited, not even after four years of dating. So why did he feel the need to emphasize she should not come?

Also, this wasn't an ordinary weekend. This was the weekend of the annual arts and crafts festival that featured some of the best wood carvers. There were carvers who made elaborate carvings of ducks, eagles, hawks and various other wildlife. Ralph always custom ordered himself something each year from the carver who won the first prize contest for best woodcarving. He prided himself on the fact he always purchased the carving that won first place or he purchased a custom order from the first place winner. Ralph's collection included a custom hand carved eagle with diamond eyes, a hawk with gold painted claws, ducks with elaborate detail work and many other unique carvings. Jasmine knew there was no way Ralph would miss a chance to add another prize-winning piece to his collection.

There were also open houses of the most expensive unusual homes in the town and people would come from all around to see the parade of homes. Ralph's home was not one of the tour homes but he felt people expected his support. In his mind, his presence was crucial to the success of the tours. Ralph would never leave town on this particular weekend.

When Jasmine asked Ralph where he was going over the weekend, Ralph said he wasn't sure. He said he had agreed to accompany a buddy of his on the long drive to North Carolina to keep him company on the road. Jasmine asked what they were going to do in North Carolina. He said he didn't know. He didn't even know where they were staying overnight.

Now Ralph is not the spontaneous type. He is a rigid planner. Ralph organizes to the point of being anal. He always knows where he is going and has an agenda of events and the time to be spent at each function. He has always needed a routine and being in his late sixties, he wasn't about to change. It just didn't add up. After four years with this man, Jasmine knew he was up to no good.

There had been times in the past Ralph had told Jasmine he couldn't see her. He was busy taking care of his business, had family visiting from out of town or any number of reasons. However, many times Jasmine would hear from friends that they had seen Ralph out on the town in Old Town Alexandria, Virginia, or in Washington, D.C. with a female and it was obviously not a friend or relative. Every time Jasmine confronted him, he would deny, deny, deny. Ralph would tell Jasmine the person who told her was either a gossip or was jealous of him. Ralph would then accuse Jasmine of being a jealous insecure woman. Many times following her confrontation, he would say he couldn't take her jealous suspicious mind and he would break up with her. After all, Jasmine had no evidence. Jasmine suspected he would use this time to try out another lady and when it didn't work out, he would come back to her to resume their relationship. Since Jasmine had no real proof, she would listen to his sweet talk, start doubting herself and end up taking him back.

Jasmine called Catherine and said she just had to know if her intuition about this weekend was right. Catherine told her to follow her gut. Women's intuition is usually right and there was no need to drive all the way to his place. But alas, Catherine knew Jasmine didn't want to believe the worst and was not going to trust her own judgment. She wouldn't cheat so why would he cheat? One thing Catherine had discovered over the years was that if a man accuses you of cheating when you are not cheating, most of the time it is because he is cheating. He cheats and therefore he suspects you will do the same. You don't cheat and therefore it is easier to believe he won't cheat.

On Saturday morning the phone rang. Catherine knew, even before looking at the Caller ID, that it was Jasmine.

"Good morning Jasmine. What time are we leaving?"

"Can you be ready in thirty minutes?"

"Yes."

"Good. I'll pick you up."

Catherine didn't want to go because she had thrown her back out of place and it was really hurting. It was an uncomfortable prospect of taking a long car ride with a hurting back but Catherine believed Ralph was cheating and felt it would be good to prove it to Jasmine. Maybe Jasmine would be able to dump Ralph for good and get him out of her system. If that happened, it would be worth the trip.

Before thirty minutes was up, Jasmine was pounding at Catherine's door, anxious to depart.

Upon opening the door, Catherine quickly glanced at Jasmine and noticed her appearance. Jasmine's short brown-layered hair, which was usually very soft, fluffy and stylish, was now tossed in different directions, looking as if she had just gotten out of bed with one half of her hair smashed to the side of her head. Although Jasmine could attend any black tie event and look like a million bucks, her daily attire would usually be described as polished casual. However, on this day, the word polished was nowhere to be found and as far as casual, even that word wasn't appropriate. She wasn't dressed the way a woman would dress who was getting ready to confront her lover and the other woman. She was wearing long tan shorts, a wrinkled tee shirt, and leopard print anklets with clogs. This was not an appealing look for Jasmine. As a matter of fact, in the fourteen years of their friendship, never before had Catherine seen Jasmine look so disheveled. For a brief moment, Catherine thought about saying something to her dear friend, but then decided otherwise. After all, what did it matter? If Ralph spoke the truth, he wouldn't be there to see Jasmine looking her worst, and if he were there, then it really wouldn't matter how she looked since they would be breaking up.

It was a long drive. They stopped at the arts and crafts fair when they arrived in town. Not to look at the merchandise, but more to feel as if they had a purpose for being there besides catching Ralph in the act. Jasmine knew there was no chance of seeing Ralph because she knew he would have gone earlier that morning. His schedule was iron clad. After a quick walk through, Jasmine and Catherine headed for Ralph's land.

Ralph's house was smack dab in the middle of three hundred and fifty acres of his own personal wild life refuge. The gate to his property had a bell that rang in the house whenever anyone opened the gate to drive onto his land. Catherine jumped out of the car and swung the gate open knowing the warning bell had been set off.

Ralph's house had many high-powered telescopes at the windows. Even though trees surrounded the property, there was one clearing where Jasmine knew Ralph could see who was coming down the dirt road. She knew he would be looking, he always did. Of course maybe he was telling the truth and was really out of town.

When they finally reached the house, Ralph was out in front waiting for their arrival. Catherine noticed he had developed a bit of a gut since the last time she had seen him. The sun was glistening off his balding head. They got out of the car and he greeted them with a big smile and arms wide open.

"Welcome. Look how lucky I am today. Two beautiful ladies visiting me. Let's go into town for some coffee."

"I thought you were going to be out of town?" Jasmine sputtered.

"My trip got cancelled at the last minute. Let's go into town and I'll tell you all about it." He was trying to coax them with his arms back to the car. It was obvious he did not want them to enter his house.

"I have to go to the rest room," Jasmine announced.

"I do too," echoed Catherine.

"You can both go at the coffee shop."

"No," Jasmine replied, "I have to go now. I can't wait any longer."

Catherine agreed she also was in dire need. Ralph told them to wait there while he straightened up the house. Before they could say anything, he quickly darted inside.

Jasmine said, "I feel sick." She knew Ralph didn't have to straighten up anything. His house was always impeccably clean with nothing ever out of place. Plus, he had a maid who came in religiously every Thursday.

"We'll know in a minute," Catherine told her.

"I think I have to throw up."

"Just take a deep breath."

Jasmine started taking deep breaths as they headed for his house.

Ralph opened the front door and softly directed, "Jasmine, you go upstairs to the rest room and Catherine you use this one," he pointed to the bathroom off the entryway. "Meet me outside as soon as you're finished."

From the bathroom Catherine could hear Ralph pacing back and forth on the stone entryway, impatiently waiting for them to appear. As soon as Jasmine came downstairs, Ralph whisked her outside. Catherine was stalling in the rest room. When she heard the front door close behind them, she headed to the living room area. They hadn't come all this way not to find out the truth and Catherine was pretty sure since Ralph sent Jasmine upstairs, the alleged lady would have to be downstairs.

As Catherine entered the living room, she spotted a lady rocking in an old oak rocking chair. The lady had a blank look on her face. She was clinching the arms of the rocking chair so hard you could see the veins in her hands bulging out. She looked to be in her late fifties to early sixties and had on tight black jeans, pointy-toed black western boots and a white cotton turtleneck sweater. She was wearing a large turquoise necklace that matched her turquoise and silver belt buckle. Her eyes were outlined with thick black liner. Her stiff beet red hair was ratted high with flipped back bangs. Her makeup was thick, accentuating her deep facial lines. She was rocking so fast back and forth that Catherine was afraid the woman would get shaken red head syndrome. Had Ralph told her to sit down and not make a sound? Was she obeying his orders? If so, then she was off her rocker. It looked as if Ralph was on the verge of being caught red-handed with a red head.

In a friendly voice Catherine said, "Hello."

"Hello," responded the red head without emotion.

"I'm Catherine McTuttle."

"Nice to meet you," she said coldly with no eye contact.

"What's your name?"

"I'm Janet."

"Nice to meet you Janet."

Catherine sat down on the sofa and started emptying her purse on the glass coffee table in front of her. Catherine explained to Janet that her back was killing her and she needed to take some medicine. It really was true but mostly just a very convenient stalling tactic.

"I found my aspirin," declared Catherine.

"Good."

"I'll be right back. I'm going to get a glass of water from the kitchen. Don't stop rocking. I know where the glasses are."

After Catherine took her aspirin, she returned to the living room and sat back down on the sofa.

"I didn't catch your last name Janet."

"I'd rather not say," she responded.

"And I thought I had a funny last name."

There was silence. Janet didn't change her blank look or the pace of her rocking. Catherine wanted to bombard Janet with questions but decided interrogating Janet might not be the best tactic.

"Are you from around here?"

"No," Janet replied, still staring straight in front of her.

"Are you Ralph's visiting relative?" Catherine asked, trying to sound casual.

"No."

"Oh, I thought you might be."

"Why would you think that?"

"He seems to have a lot of female relatives that visit."

For the first time, Janet looked directly at Catherine with a glare that would have made the devil proud. Catherine became immediately uncomfortable and decided not to continue her line of questioning. It was obvious Janet was not going to be forthcoming with any information.

In the meantime, Ralph came in and was upset to find Catherine in the living room. "What are you doing in here? Jasmine is waiting outside. You need to leave now," he bellowed.

Catherine explained she would leave as soon as she put everything back in her purse. She was taking her sweet time organizing everything and was almost through when she heard the front door open.

"Jasmine, we're in here," Catherine quickly sang.

Ralph shot Catherine an evil look. He was visibly upset with her. Could you blame him? He was about to be officially busted. Years before Ralph had nicknamed Catherine, "the bad seed," and she was finally living up to her reputation. Of course, she wasn't really the cause of the trouble that was about to erupt. Ralph had done this to himself. But a man like Ralph never holds himself accountable.

When Jasmine came in and saw Janet, the look on Jasmine's face was heartbreaking. Catherine saw the torment her best friend was now feeling. She knew even though Jasmine had suspected another woman, it was a very different matter to have the other woman right in front of you. Ralph had obviously not confessed to any wrongdoing when he was outside with Jasmine. It was evident Jasmine was not expecting to see another woman in his house.

To break the awkward silence, Catherine decided to introduce the two ladies. "Jasmine Wakefield, this is Janet Wouldrathernotsay."

Neither woman exchanged greetings. Jasmine studied the woman before her in the rocking chair. Janet kept up her pace of rocking and sat there with a blank look on her face, still clutching the armrest as if to keep herself from flying off.

Catherine noticed an elaborately carved hawk with broad, rounded wings and a long tail, displayed on top of the bookcase behind Ralph. She wondered how many times the hawk had looked down upon Ralph's prey.

Jasmine walked towards Janet, standing a few feet in front of her. Suddenly, Jasmine pointed her forefinger at Janet and scolded, "I want you to remember this day. Remember what I'm telling you. When you want to get rid of this man, and believe me, the day will come when you want to get rid of him, you'll have to do something to make him leave you alone. You'll need to confront him. Catch him. That's the only way. Otherwise you'll end up hearing nothing but lie after lie from him. He'll string you along for his own amusement. He'll want to keep you in the picture, along with others. You may be the main woman in his life but I guarantee you won't ever be the only woman. Don't kid yourself. He is a liar, a womanizer, a cad, deceitful, and did I say womanizer?"

Catherine responded, "You already said womanizer."

Ralph shot Catherine another harsh look.

Looking at Ralph, Catherine said, "Well she did. She'd already said womanizer."

Ralph maintained his glare at Catherine.

Jasmine continued, "He is a womanizer. If you don't know it now, you will and when your time comes in the future, and believe me, it will come, you'll remember this conversation. What a fool I've been. Well, you get my title now. And when you want to pass the crown to the next victim, you might want to remember the only way to discard him is to catch him in one of his lies. It'll help you move on. I'm being honest. You don't know it now. He'll have some excuse after we leave, but I'm telling the truth!"

Jasmine's voice was now almost hysterical. Tears were rolling down her cheeks. "He is a cheat. He is a womanizer. A lying, sneaky womanizer. Someday you will look back on this day and you'll understand. Then you'll know I was giving you an honest warning. I was being your friend. I don't even want to be your friend but I'm being one. Do you hear me?"

Janet said nothing as she stared off into space, giving Jasmine no eye contact.

Jasmine had now gone into what men like to refer to as, "crazy mode." Yes she was definitely in crazy mode. The thing about crazy mode is that it does happen. Women like to deny it but it's true. It is an easy possibility when dating. Men love it when it happens because they now have an excuse to dump you. After all, you are crazy! But what they conveniently leave out when repeating to their friends how crazy you were, is the series of events that took place to drive you temporarily into crazy mode. They leave out all the lies and deceitfulness, abuse of trust, all the things they did to betray you and the reason that brought you to crazy mode in the first place. Well, Catherine's best friend was now having a full-fledged case of crazy mode.

Janet sat expressionless, continuing to quickly rock back and forth, not saying a word. Jasmine stood silently in front of Janet with her forefinger still pointed at her in a warning manner. Ralph stood in the entryway of the room with his mouth wide open. Oh, what Catherine would have given for a fly to come by at that moment.

Catherine looked on the end table next to the sofa and noticed a brown hand-carved bald eagle with a beautiful white head, neck and tail. The eagle seemed to be watching the events of the moment unfolding before his keen sight. It dawned on Catherine that her friend Jasmine was finally seeing Ralph as sharply as the bald eagle sees. Only why did Catherine have the vision of a buzzard circling above the head of her wounded friend Jasmine? Catherine wondered if the buzzard was circling over Janet or was Janet happy to see her competition eliminated?

Finally the silence was broken as Ralph commanded in a stern voice, "All right Jasmine. That's about enough. Out! This is very uncomfortable. It's time for you to go."

Catherine looked at Ralph and said, "I bet it is uncomfortable. It's uncomfortable being caught in a lie. Why do you lie so much?"

"That's it," he yelled. "Jasmine, you and the bad seed out now!"

Catherine could tell he meant business. She grabbed her purse and guided Jasmine towards the front door. Jasmine was shaking all over and her face was red.

Ralph rapidly went to the front door and held it open. As they walked out the door, Jasmine still had her finger pointed just as she did when she was standing in front of Janet. Catherine wondered if Jasmine was in some kind of trance or shock.

The minute they were outside, the front door slammed shut. Catherine heard Ralph quickly turn the dead bolt lock.

Once they drove off his land, Jasmine said she needed to stop for something to drink. Her body was shaking and Catherine could tell Jasmine was not feeling well. They had passed a little café right down the road and decided it would be a good place to stop. An uncomfortable silence was in the car as they drove.

A minute later they pulled into the café parking lot and went inside. Catherine bought a mineral water and Jasmine purchased a diet coke. They took their drinks outside and sat at a small cast iron table.

Jasmine was still shaking. She looked at Catherine with tears in her eyes and said, "I did something bad."

At that moment all kinds of thoughts raced through Catherine's mind. What had Jasmine done? Did she destroy something of value in Ralph's house when she was upstairs? To what did she just make her an accomplice? Whatever it was, were they going to end up in court over it? Okay, brace yourself; it can't be that bad. Jasmine is a good person. "Oh please Lord, don't let us have to hire an attorney for anything," Catherine prayed.

Calmly, Catherine asked, "What did you do Jasmine?"

Without saying a word, Jasmine opened her purse and handed Catherine a prescription bottle.

"What's this?" Catherine asked.

Jasmine did not answer.

Catherine read the label, which said *Viagra*. Surprised she asked, "You stole his Viagra?"

Jasmine looked down and nodded her head yes. Tears were now rolling down Jasmine's cheeks from her bloodshot eyes.

Catherine started laughing, "You stole his Viagra? This is great. This is a classic. This is the perfect revenge. Jasmine, you're a genius! I bow to you oh great one. Your cleverness will be remembered always."

Jasmine looked up as a smile started creeping in even as her tears were rolling over one side of her mouth. Catherine kept laughing and soon Jasmine joined her.

"It is kind of perfect isn't it?" Jasmine said timidly.

"Are you kidding? Women all over the world will light candles in your honor. This is truly the ultimate revenge. You couldn't have done anything more perfect to get even with him."

The mood had now changed, as Jasmine appeared more relaxed. They got back in the car to drive home.

On the way, Catherine recapped everything Jasmine had said to Janet.

Jasmine had no memory of it and kept saying, "I did? Did I say that?" She was now out of crazy mode and laughing about the afternoon's events.

Catherine joked, "It's a good thing you had your nails manicured since you kept pointing that finger at Janet." Jasmine had no recollection of doing that either.

Jasmine said Ralph wouldn't miss the Viagra until evening. She knew his routine so well and knew the routine wouldn't vary from the past. She knew he and Janet had already been to the craft show and would go to the home show later that afternoon. After the home show they would go back to his place to freshen up, shower and get dressed for dinner. He would have made reservations at the Four & Twenty Black Birds restaurant, which was known for great food and a romantic setting hidden in the countryside of Virginia. It was one of his favorites and a routine event for him to go there every year at this time. After dinner they would go back to his place and take a walk around the lake. They would stop at a special bench, which Ralph had carved, and watch the geese as the sun set. As he sat with his arm around Janet, Ralph would talk about how beautiful his property is at this time of night. She should be properly impressed with his land and his wealth by now. In his mind, the romantic mood of the evening was in full motion. At the appropriate time, they would walk back and have a late night drink on the circular porch that surrounded his house as they watched the moonlight glistening off the lake.

Later, he would light a fire in the fireplace and then put on some romantic music for dancing, while kissing her softly. He would continue to fill her glass with wine. When the mood was right, he would excuse himself for a moment and go upstairs. At this point, he would rinse his mouth with toothpaste, dab on a bit of cologne, take his Viagra and be ready to slowly move in for the kill.

Oops! Wait a minute. Did I say take his Viagra? My mistake. There is no Viagra. What is poor Ralph going to do?

This is the part Catherine wished she and Jasmine could witness. They both wanted to see the look on Ralph's face when he realized his Viagra was not where it belonged. Ralph's the type of man who keeps everything is in its place. Even so, they still imagined his panic as he checked in both medicine cabinets, on the floor, under the sink, everywhere, until it dawns on him, "Jasmine and the bad seed!" Now granted, even though Catherine was not the one to go upstairs to the rest room, she's still the bad seed so she'll be blamed. He'll probably think she planted the idea in Jasmine's head or snuck upstairs when he was outside with Jasmine.

Poor, poor Ralph. What will he do? It will be too late to go to the pharmacy. Everything would be closed and he lives out in the boonies. Jasmine knew Ralph would never admit to his latest woman that he needed help and it was gone. As a matter of fact, on more than one occasion, he had mentioned to Jasmine he was a virile man and would never need to use Viagra.

It was three years ago when Jasmine woke with a headache and in her search for an aspirin, stumbled across his prescription bottle. It didn't matter to her if he was taking Viagra. However, not wanting to embarrass a very proud man, she kept that knowledge to herself.

Catherine and Jasmine thought of all the different scenarios he would use to get out of having sex. He could tell Janet he has too much respect for her to do anything with her so soon. But what if this isn't their first time? Then he'd have to use a different approach. How about he is still so shaken up from Jasmine and the bad seed that he just can't perform? No, that wouldn't be his type of approach. How about he is dead tired? Or, how about the insecure man approach? He cuts Janet down. She isn't good looking enough. She isn't thin enough. She isn't young enough. Basically, she just isn't doing it for him. Both Jasmine and Catherine would be ecstatic over any of those outcomes. It was a win-win situation as far as they were concerned.

They laughed and laughed on their return trip. Jasmine was finally over this man. After a four-year roller coaster ride, she was ready to move forward. She had caught him red handed, or red headed, and could now see the light of her salvation. For the first time in years, Jasmine felt relieved and was ready to move on with her life without Ralph.

On the way home, Jasmine asked, "What about the Viagra? What should I do with it?"

"Destroy the evidence," Catherine replied dramatically.

Catherine retrieved the Viagra out of Jasmine's purse, rolled down the window, flung open the bottle top and threw the pills to the wind. Out they went into a nearby pasture filled with livestock. There were some very happy bulls that night.

As for Ralph, Jasmine heard through the grapevine it hadn't worked out with him and Janet Wouldrathernotsay. Jasmine suspects Ralph just couldn't rise to the occasion.

I COULD JUST CROAK

Catherine's girlfriend Miriam was going to a private black tie function in Washington, D.C. Miriam's ex-husband, Ted, whom Miriam had not seen for many years, was going to be there with his new young wife. As many wealthy men do, Ted had married a lady twenty years younger than himself. Miriam wondered if Ted understood that if his money ever disappeared, so would his darling new wife. Miriam was sure Ted's inflated ego would not let him see the truth.

This black tie function was not an event to attend alone and Miriam was not dating anyone. She could not show up for an evening of dinner and dancing by herself. It was just too humiliating. It wasn't that she wanted Ted back. Miriam had divorced him and had no regrets. It's just that it would be embarrassing to show up stag and he would have his darling young wife with him. In her eyes, he was the loser, who remarried, and here she was still single. She didn't mind being single; she just didn't want to be single in front of him.

Catherine told Miriam there was no shame in going alone. After all, it just proved she was a secure woman who could stand on her own. Miriam still wanted to have someone go with her, and truthfully, Catherine would have too. Who wants to go to a couples event and be the lone wallflower watching all the other couples dance? And besides, Miriam's ex-husband was going to be there flaunting his youthful new bride.

Miriam RSVP'd for two and decided she would make a conscious effort to get herself out there to find someone. She also called all her friends to see if they knew of anyone decent to escort her, but no luck.

Catherine agreed to rack her brain and try to think of someone worthwhile for Miriam. Surely with all the women friends Miriam had, someone would be able to think of one good man to accompany her to this event.

It was now the week before the function and Miriam found herself panicking. Time was ticking away.

Finally, Catherine thought of someone Miriam could take to the event. His name was Randy and he was successful, tall, handsome, looked fantastic in his tuxedo and would be the perfect man to chaperon Miriam. Catherine called Randy and he said he was free that night and would be delighted to escort Miriam. He even said he would pretend they were an item and very serious, which was something Miriam said she wished could happen. Catherine called Miriam immediately, so excited to tell her she had no more worries. Catherine knew Miriam would be thrilled because Randy was the perfect escort. To Catherine's surprise, Miriam politely declined.

Miriam explained she had been in the bookstore and was approached by an attractive man named Brad. He was twelve years younger than Miriam. She told Catherine she and Brad talked for about thirty minutes and he seemed very presentable. Miriam asked him if he owned a tuxedo and if he was available for a really nice function that coming weekend. Brad said yes on both counts.

Catherine told Miriam she really felt she would be better off with Randy since she had known him for years and he was truly a class act. Besides, she had only talked to Brad for a short amount of time.

Miriam declined her offer stating she had already asked Brad to accompany her and thought the evening would be great fun. Miriam had told Brad about Ted and that a lot of Ted's stuffy friends were going to be at the black tie dinner. Brad had agreed to act as if he and Miriam were an item. Miriam said he was really a sport about everything and she thought there might be great potential for a future with him. Miriam felt her worries were over.

Catherine called Miriam late in the afternoon on the day of the party to see how everything was going. Miriam had gotten a manicure, pedicure, facial, bought an elegant new gown and had her hair styled. She said she looked and felt beautiful. Catherine knew it was true.

Miriam was a petite attractive brunette and when she fixed up, she was a knockout.

Miriam was now looking forward to the evening she had been dreading before young Brad came into her life. Miriam agreed she would call Catherine first thing in the morning to share the details of the party. Miriam was confident it would be an evening to remember.

The next morning Miriam called to tell her about the evening's events. Miriam said for some reason the place cards had Brad and her sitting at the same table as Ted and his young new wife. As a matter of fact, it was a round table and Ted sat directly across from her. She wondered if this was just a coincidence or planned by her ex-husband and his friends. Anyway, Miriam said Ted's wife was adorable and Ted was doting all over her as if she were his new prize.

Miriam was pleased with Brad's handsome appearance in his tuxedo. Brad had a deep rich tan that looked great with his blondish-brown streaked hair. He was young and healthy with his athletic body showing off his broad shoulders and thin waist. She was sure he had a defined washboard stomach, an assumption she hoped to research later.

Miriam felt at first, the evening went fairly well. Brad played up that he and Miriam had been seeing each other for quite some time and to Miriam's delight, even announced to the table they were considering marriage in the near future. Brad made it sound as if he and Miriam were inseparable. Miriam noticed her ex-husband Ted seemed to have a change in his mood after the news she might be wedding. Ted always was the type who wanted what he couldn't have and the wedding announcement by Brad proved Ted hadn't changed one bit, which pleased Miriam to no end.

They had made it through appetizers of blue crab soup and a spinach salad with champagne dressing when the waiter brought out the entrées. Miriam ordered the duck breast roasted with wild thyme accompanied by new red potatoes. Brad's dinner was grilled prime rib beef with garlic mashed potatoes and asparagus.

Everything was going smoothly. The table conversation was easily flowing with a polite discussion of current events regarding Washington politics. Miriam was thrilled. She even caught a sad puppy dog glimpse from Ted, which was an additional bonus to the evening. A smug feeling overcame her as she enjoyed her victorious dinner. However, this smug feeling was short lived. They were half way through the entrée when Brad commenced coughing. He kept coughing until everyone at the table stopped talking and started looking at him with great concern.

"I think he's choking," one of the ladies yelled.

"Oh my God, somebody do something," another lady screamed in a panic.

Just then Brad stood up, grabbed his throat with both hands, knocked his chair over and dropped to the floor. Everyone at the table gasped as they jumped up in alarm and ran to Brad's aid. While Brad was lying on the floor he brought both of his hands over his mouth, made one final loud cough and up from his hands popped a green plastic frog.

Brad grinned and said, "I guess I had a frog in my throat."

Miriam studied the goofy grin on Brad's face. "What's going on Brad? Was this a joke?"

"Hey, someone had to break the ice. You were right. What a stuffy group of people at this event."

Miriam said all heads turned from looking at Brad on the floor to looking at her. It took her a moment to realize Brad had actually planned the whole episode as a joke. Could this really be happening? Miriam felt the cold stares from the group of people whom moment's earlier, she knew she had been impressing. She was positive they were now thinking, "So this is the man you are going to marry." Miriam felt humiliated. Without saying a word she grabbed her purse and dashed out of the banquet room.

Brad picked up his green plastic frog, probably to save for the next black tie event, and ran after her.

On the way home, Miriam told Brad she was so embarrassed he would do something so juvenile. She wanted to know how he could have possibly thought his actions were going to be funny or even the least bit appropriate. Miriam said as she scolded Brad, he sat there expressionless with no response to her tongue-lashing. The rest of the way home, there was silence in the car since he apparently had nothing to say, which suited her fine.

When they pulled up in front of her house, Brad told Miriam they were never going to work out because she obviously did not have a sense of humor. He said he was very disappointed to find she was such a cold humorless person.

Miriam jumped out of Brad's car, slamming his car door behind her. She had nothing more to say to Brad. No words could fix her humiliated feelings. That was the last time Miriam and Brad ever spoke.

As Miriam unfolded the events of her disastrous evening, Catherine wished she could have seen it on video. Catherine reminded Miriam that a year from now they were going to be sitting around laughing about her evening out. Miriam didn't find any of it amusing because it was still too fresh.

Catherine told Miriam she was sure this wasn't the first time Brad had pulled this frog stunt. She was sure when he was in grade school, this trick went over really well in the cafeteria. His buddies were probably looking on and laughing as Brad preformed at the girls' lunch table.

Several months later for Miriam's birthday, Catherine bought her a big green rubber frog that went, "croak, croak, croak," every time you squeezed its stomach.

Miriam finally laughed.

THE SHOE'S ON THE OTHER FOOT

One day, Katie was at a pool party when a tall, lean, unimposing man approached her. He had thinning blonde hair and a fair complexion. Through visiting, Katie found out his name was Gerald, he was a forty-nine year old dentist, loved movies, lived in a modern home in the country and had never been married.

Katie was with a group of friends and they were on their way out the door so she had to cut their conversation short, but Gerald made sure Katie had his business card before she left. Although it wasn't necessary, Gerald encouraged Katie to call him, stating he was very interested in getting to know her.

A few days later Katie called Gerald. He told her about his dental practice and about his new custom-built home with its own home theatre. He asked her about her life, and the things she liked to do. They talked for a while and he seemed very nice so they made plans to go to dinner and a movie the following Saturday night.

Saturday evening turned out to be a very hot summer evening. Katie put on a casual pale yellow flowered sundress and some summer slip on shoes.

Gerald picked Katie up at her house and drove her to Clyde's at Reston Town Center for dinner. The movie theatre was just down the block from the restaurant so it was really convenient to walk to the movies after dinner.

When they arrived at the restaurant, they were seated at a booth. As soon as they sat down, Gerald took his shoes off and stretched his long legs out, putting his bare feet on Katie's side of the booth. He told her he hated to wear shoes and he felt more people should learn to relax. He said it wasn't natural for people to wear shoes. As he explained it, "Feet like to breathe."

Katie felt fortunate his large sockless feet didn't smell since they were right next to her. She was also glad he didn't need other parts of his body to breathe. She found herself especially turned off because even though she did her best not to glance at his feet, she couldn't help but notice his toenails were long and yellow and his feet were callused. She could have done without that visual.

During dinner, Gerald dropped his napkin. A moment later Katie felt him grab her leg and quickly slip off one of her shoes. When she protested and pulled the other foot back, he came up from under the booth.

"Come on. Get comfortable."

"No, I like wearing shoes. I want my shoe back."

"It's not going to happen. Come on, take the other shoe off and get comfortable," he insisted.

"I'm not the barefoot type."

"You are now. Admit it, doesn't it feel great?"

"No, really, I don't like going barefoot. We're in a public place too. If I don't go barefoot at home, I'm certainly not going barefoot in a restaurant."

"You'll get over it. Besides, if you're honest, you'll admit you like it."

The more Katie insisted the more determined Gerald seemed to be to keep her shoe. She decided being mad wasn't going to work. She needed another tactic. She started asking him questions about what he liked and found he had a television in every room in the house so he could be watching one show and walk from room to room and never miss a segment of any program. He also had a generator hooked up so if the electricity ever went out, he would have a back up power source. The generator wasn't for lighting, heat or anything practical. He said he needed to insure he would never be without a television. He threw parties where all his friends could come to his movie theatre and watch football.

As he explained, "You never have to worry about entertaining anyone when you have a movie theatre. It's great for dating too, no talking necessary."

Katie was wishing she had a remote control she could point at Gerald and change dates.

After talking for a while, Katie told Gerald she had to use the rest room. She started to get up and then declared she had to have her shoe because it was unsanitary to go in a rest room without wearing shoes. She would have mentioned it was also uncomfortable to walk with only one shoe, but she was afraid Gerald would insist on taking her other shoe. Her plan worked because Gerald returned her shoe. When she returned from the restroom, she was very guarded about the location of her feet. Luckily, Gerald did not attempt to take her shoe again, which was a relief.

After dinner Katie and Gerald walked to the movies. While they were standing in line, he started talking to a group of high school girls who were in front of him. He kept interrupting their conversation trying to be funny. It was obvious the girls wanted nothing to do with him but they were being polite. Gerald started telling them stupid jokes and when he finished laughing at his jokes, Katie could see the girls glance at each other and roll their eyes. Katie was embarrassed he was her date. She again wished she had a remote control so she could hit mute.

As soon as they sat down in the movie theatre, Gerald took off his shoes again. It was disgusting that his bare feet were on a public movie theatre floor. She wondered if the floor felt sticky and if it did, would he even notice or care? He was in an aisle seat and when the movie started, he stretched one of his long legs into the aisle. Katie was even more repulsed by him now and she was determined to keep her feet as far away from him as possible in case he decided she should join him in his barefoot escapade. The plan was to wear her shoes during the entire movie, and the thought of sitting there guarding the position of her feet was ridiculous. Nevertheless, she made sure they were out of Gerald's reach. Luckily, he left her shoes alone.

On the drive home Gerald said he was hurt because Katie had sat with her arms crossed during the entire movie and he really wanted to hold her hand. He said he sensed something was wrong and wanted to know if he was correct.

Katie didn't feel like telling him she found him disgusting. Her motto has always been if you think someone might be worth it, then you should talk through things. However, in this case, she wasn't interested and saw no advantage to discussing how she felt about him. Katie's perception of him was he was immature, lacked class, and was a repulsive man. Obviously, that was best kept to herself.

As they drove down the street, Gerald asked, "How about another date?"

Katie hated being put on the spot, especially when he just paid for dinner and a movie. She had no intention of going out with him again.

"I'll need to check my calendar and get back with you," she said as a stalling tactic.

"Are you saying that to put me off? I'd appreciate your being honest with me. Do you want to go out again?"

"I've got to check on dates and let you know."

"I'll tell you what, why don't you pick any day in the next few weeks you're available. We'll go out then. You could come over and see my home theatre."

"Oh right. I could watch television from any room."

"Yes you can. But you'll love the home theatre. You must know of one day you're free without checking your calendar. Everyone has one day with no plans."

Katie could tell he wasn't willing to give her an easy out. For a moment, she thought about picking a date and then canceling later. She really didn't want to go down that path. She visualized herself pointing a television remote control at him and hitting all the buttons for a change. Previous channel, mute, even static would be an improvement.

"Look. You're a nice man but we just aren't a good match."

"Based on what?"

"Based on the way I feel."

"What does that mean?"

"It means we aren't compatible. If one person feels it isn't a good match, then the relationship won't work."

By now they were a few blocks from her house. Gerald was livid with Katie's response. Quickly he jerked the car over to the curb, reached across her and flung her car door open.

"Get out!" he demanded.

Katie thought it was a perfect touch to confirm what she already knew. She stepped out of the car.

Gerald quickly slammed the door behind her and sped off, squealing his tires.

Katie was happy to be away from him. As she walked the rest of the way to her house, she looked down at the sidewalk and spotted some broken glass. Katie thought, "How nice it is to be wearing my shoes."

FLAWLES

One day after work Catherine stopped at the library to pick up a back-ordered book. That's when she ran into Ellen, whom she hadn't seen for years, not since their daughters sang in the church choir together. Catherine and Ellen chatted as they walked out to the parking lot. Ellen said she and her husband Martin were moving back to Chicago where both of them had family. Martin had acquired a new position in a law firm and they would be moving within two weeks. Ellen was sorry to be leaving all her friends behind but excited about their move.

"Are you dating anyone special?" asked Ellen.

"Always dating someone, never dating anyone," Catherine laughed.

"Oh, I have the perfect man for you. His name is James Gordon."

Ellen told Catherine that James was tall, handsome, mature and very well educated. He graduated summa cum laude from Boston College and went to Harvard Law School. As Ellen said, "He's a very impressive man." Ellen explained James had been divorced around five years, and his wife had cheated on him. She told Catherine James said he hated the singles scene and really wanted someone special. Ellen guessed his age to be around mid sixties. She said he traveled internationally for his job and he had told her he really wished he had someone to accompany him on his travels. "I think he's ready for a wife. He hates being alone."

Ellen stated James had the most interesting stories from his travels. She said he continually traveled to Europe, Latin America, the Middle East and Asia. She confessed she honestly didn't know him that well but from their few meetings, she was very impressed. Ellen asked Catherine if she was willing to be fixed up.

"Of course!" Catherine quickly replied. Catherine trusted Ellen's judgment in men since Ellen had a fantastic husband. "This man sounds perfect."

In the past, when Catherine had been fixed up on a date, those dates had not turned out well. However, her Mom and Dad met on a blind date and they'd been married for over fifty years. Catherine gave Ellen her phone number and told her to have James call if he was interested.

That night James Gordon called. He had a low pleasant voice. Catherine didn't talk very long with James because he had just gotten back from an overseas trip and was exhausted. They made plans to go out to dinner on Saturday night.

Late on Saturday afternoon Catherine received a call from James. He sounded terrible. He had the flu with a fever of 102 degrees. He said every bone in his body was aching.

"Do you have medicine?" Catherine asked.

"Yes. But I don't have any food in the house."

"I'd be happy to bring by some chicken noodle soup."

"Thanks but no thanks. No way do I want you to see me. I look terrible and don't want to get dressed."

Catherine assured him he shouldn't be concerned, she would leave it on the front porch, ring the bell so he knew the food had arrived, and depart. They would never see each other.

James agreed to accept the soup under those conditions. He then gave Catherine directions to his house.

About two minutes later Catherine was on her way out the door when the phone rang. It was James. "You're not going to give me any of that canned stuff are you? I want something good."

"No. I'm going to pick up some soup at Chicken Out. They have great chicken noodle soup there."

"Okay."

Catherine thought it was rude of him to call back with that question, but she chalked it up to him being sick.

James lived in Great Falls, Virginia. Driving to his place took a lot longer than Catherine had anticipated due to the slick winding roads. The rain was coming down heavy, making it difficult to see, plus it was turning dark outside, which just added to the stressful drive. The traffic was terrible. By the time Catherine reached his neighborhood, more than two hours had passed since she had walked out her front door.

As Catherine turned onto his street, she was impressed with the homes. Beautiful mansions with massive yards surrounded by tall lean oak and walnut trees. Catherine spotted his house number on the mailbox at the road and pulled in his drive. Two large stone lions adorned each side of the driveway entrance. Catherine could see his house on a hill directly in front of her. It reminded her of the architecture of Monticello with its white columns in front.

It was still pouring rain when Catherine jumped out of her car and ran to his front porch. She left the bag, which was filled with a large chicken noodle soup, enough for several meals, a baguette, creamed spinach, a large mineral water and three big chocolate chip cookies. Catherine rang the doorbell and ran back to her car. She'd done her good deed for the day and was sure her efforts would be appreciated.

James called her three days later and said he was feeling much better. He was leaving town to go to London in a few days and would be tied up getting things caught up at the office until his departure. He promised he would call her immediately upon his return from London and they would definitely get together. James explained he would be gone anywhere from three weeks to two months depending on how quickly he wrapped up his business. He apologized and said he really wished he could see her before he left but he just couldn't work it into his schedule. He said he was e-mailing her a picture of himself so he wouldn't seem like such a stranger upon his return. James requested a picture of her to take with him on his trip. Catherine promised she'd do her best to find one.

In the background Catherine could hear dogs yapping. In baby talk, she heard James say, "I hear you sweethearts. Daddy will be off the phone in a minute." Then he explained, "I have three little precious ones that you'll have to meet. Their names are Miss Sunshine, Miss Poison and Miss Ivy." He told her they were Yorkshire Terriers. He added, "Miss Sunshine is warming herself in a ray of sunlight. She loves to sunbathe."

James told Catherine he had driven to Canada to get one Yorkshire Terrier from an excellent breeder. Miss Sunshine was the first one he saw and she immediately lit up his life, which of course is why he named her Miss Sunshine. Then he saw Miss Poison and Miss Ivy. The breeder told James they never left each other's side. He saw a mischievous gleam in their eyes and knew they wanted him for their daddy. James expressed, "I've never been one to disappoint the ladies." James said the other dogs didn't stand out, "They just looked like dogs." He got the three, "special ones."

Miss Sunshine, Miss Poison and Miss Ivy kept yapping as James continued with his story about them. He spoke to them again in baby talk. "Okay, okay. Daddy will get off the phone." He noted they get jealous when they don't have his attention. He prattled on, "They don't like it when Daddy talks on the phone. Daddy's going to get off now. Yes I am. Yes I am my little darlings. Daddy knows what his girls want."

Catherine had never talked baby talk to her daughter Molly, not even when Molly was a baby. As unappealing as his baby talk sounded, she chuckled to herself thinking it also showed a very sweet side to James. Catherine and James said goodbye and agreed they would get together upon his return.

Catherine had a favorite picture of her daughter Molly and herself she had taken about six months earlier. For years Catherine had wanted a picture of the two of them but they just hadn't taken the time to get a family photo. Catherine had plenty of shots of Molly but none of the two of them. One day Catherine told Molly she had ten minutes to get ready because she was going to take a family photo. When Molly came outside, Catherine set the automatic timer on the camera and ran to get in the picture frame. It's funny how such a spur of the moment shot could come out so perfect. They were leaning against their ranch style fence in the front yard with the background a blur of trees. Not a strand of their long blonde hair was out of place and the picture captured their friendly smiles. They were dressed very casual. Catherine was wearing jeans with a light pink top that looked great with her pearls and Molly wore a soft blue top with her favorite gold necklace and a cute denim skirt. It was a great easygoing shot.

Catherine removed the picture out of the frame and took it to the corner shop to make a copy for James. She made the picture wallet size so James would have the option of taking it with him. Catherine went straight to the post office to insure James would receive it before departing on his trip.

The day before he left, Catherine received a voice mail message from James saying he received the picture and thought she was beautiful. He couldn't wait to spend time with her upon his return.

A few days later Catherine received a package in the mail. It was an eleven by fourteen picture of James with a note saying, "Decided not to send an e-mail. Original photo, better for framing." He looked much younger than she had visualized. He actually looked to be around forty years old so Catherine figured it must be an old picture or he really looked young for his age. The package also included his biography at the law firm. He had a very impressive bio along with his very large picture.

About two weeks later Catherine came home from work to find a voice mail message from James. "I need you to do me a favor. I'm thinking about buying a painting and having it shipped over. Get a tape measure and go to my house. Go to the iron gate at the side of the garage. Go through to the backyard to the pool house. The pool house door is unlocked. Go in the pool house. There is a big walk-in closet to your right. Go into the closet and reach above the door where you'll find a key on the inside ledge. Take the key because you'll need it to open the side garage door. Go in the garage. The door from the garage to the house is unlocked and the alarm is off. I've had a workman coming in and out so I've had to keep the alarm off." Catherine was then instructed to go to the dining room. "There is one wall that has nothing on it, no painting, nothing. Measure that wall and be sure to get the exact measurements. Don't measure the floorboard or the crown molding, only measure the wall space. This is a very large painting and I must know that it will fit exactly the way I want it to so be sure to measure it accurately. Do it twice to verify you have the correct measurements. Leave me a voice mail message on my home number with the information. I'll be checking my messages daily. Oh, by the way, I've sent you a few post cards. You probably don't have them yet, but you should soon. I really wish you were here. I can't wait for us to meet."

Since Catherine really didn't know James, she wondered why he would ask her to measure his wall. Didn't he have any friends, neighbors or even the workman who already had access to his house who could perform this task for him? Even though she thought it was bizarre he called her, she really didn't mind. Her curiosity to inspect the inside of his house was suddenly overwhelming. This was an opportunity she wasn't going to miss. His mansion was so beautiful from the outside that she knew she wouldn't be disappointed. Excited to start her new adventure, she called her friend Jasmine and requested she go with her right away to his house. Besides, Catherine really did need someone to help her hold the tape measure. It was a much easier job with two people.

Jasmine was more than eager to accompany Catherine because she too was curious to view the inside of his home.

Catherine and Jasmine followed his instructions to a T but the door from the garage to the house was locked. They could only get as far as the garage so their adventure of seeing his house wasn't going to happen. Catherine called her home voice mail messages from her cell phone to listen to his instructions one more time; just in case she had missed something, but she found they had followed his instructions perfectly.

Jasmine and Catherine were really impressed with the maintenance it took to keep up his yard. It must have required a full time crew. The lawn was very formal with paths winding around clipped yew and box hedges. It was a very romantic setting, but a little too formal for Catherine's taste. She enjoyed more of a wilderness view and yet she appreciated the beauty of his property. The estate itself was surrounded by wilderness with its tall Virginia trees, but his yard was meticulously cared for with every inch a production in beauty. There were azaleas lining the house with vines crawling up a trellis, which extended to the second floor. It was elegant everywhere they looked.

A stone terrace was at the rear of the house and had bronze fountains on each corner. There were large steps from the terrace leading down to the tiled pool. Large marble statues on top of stone columns adorned each corner of the pool and there was even a little fountain in the center of the stone courtyard to the side of the swimming pool. An iron fence with ivy clinging to it surrounded the massive pool area. The pool house was as big as both their homes and very plush. Jasmine and Catherine decided they would be content living in the pool house. They fantasized about how nice it would be but of course in their fantasy they had many male servants who catered to their every whim. With or without servants, the place was a touch of paradise.

When Catherine got home, she left a message for James that the door to the house was locked so she couldn't enter. At least she tried.

The next day, Catherine returned home from work to find a message from James. He stated, "One hundred percent that door was open." James explained his workman needed to get in and out to do his job and he, James, specifically remembered double-checking the door before he left town to be sure it was unlocked. James said to forget about it. He would get someone else to go in and measure the wall space.

Over the next few weeks Catherine received several nice postcards from James. Each one was sweeter than the previous. Some of them were very funny too. He had sent several that showed a picture of his hotel with a window of the hotel circled, indicating the location of his room. Then one day Catherine received a postcard with a park bench circled. The post card read, "The hotel was full. Met a really nice man and he shared his brown paper bag." Catherine thought it was kind of cute and showed a sense of humor.

One day Catherine came home from work to find a large white basket filled with flowers. The attached note read, "Looking forward to seeing you upon my return." She responded with a voice mail thanking him for the flowers and telling him she too was looking forward to getting together with him.

When James returned from London, he called and explained he was exhausted and desperately needed to catch up on his sleep. James said he preferred talking in person rather than on the phone so would love to get together with Catherine. It was a quick call but they made plans for the following Saturday night. He told Catherine to leave the afternoon and evening open so they could make a day of it because he really wanted to spend as much time with her as possible to make up for all the time they spent apart. Catherine was both flattered and excited.

On Friday night James called to confirm their plans. He wanted to pick Catherine up around three o'clock and drive to Leesburg, Virginia to go antique shopping in the afternoon. He continued to say he had made reservations at a very nice restaurant for that evening.

Catherine loved antiques and had never been to Leesburg so was thrilled at the day James had planned. She was really looking forward to meeting James Gordon. For the brief moment they spoke on the phone, he sounded so mature. That was exactly what she wanted in a man. Plus it sounded like a fun day. Beautiful weather had been predicted for Saturday and the thought of spending the day walking around the streets of Leesburg going in and out of little antique shops was very appealing. Maybe she'd even be able to add another interesting antique candleholder to her collection.

On Saturday morning, Catherine rose early, unable to sleep due to her anticipation of finally meeting James. She took a shower, threw on some jeans, a camisole with a lightweight yellow sweater and headed to the salon. She had made an appointment with one of the most expensive stylists, but felt it was worth the money. She wanted to look fantastic for James.

Three hours later, she departed the salon $350.00 poorer but with a manicure, pedicure and freshly highlighted blonde streaks in her long hair. Her hair was now glistening with a smooth, silky texture.

When Catherine arrived home she pulled out a spaghetti-strapped long black dress that could easily go from dressy casual during the afternoon to dressy for the evening. This was the evening for her best jewelry so she accessorized with her favorite diamond earrings and a small diamond necklace. When she looked in the mirror she thought, "I look so good, I'd date me." She was having a very good hair, face and clothes day. Since that doesn't always happen, she really appreciated it happening on this particular day.

At three o'clock Catherine was ready and waiting, watching for James through the front window. However, instead of him pulling up in the driveway, the phone rang with James on the other end. He said he was in the middle of working on a project and couldn't get away. He was going to be running really late and said it would be more like six o'clock before he could make it to her place.

Catherine hid her disappointment from James by stating, "Take your time. I've got plenty to keep me busy. There's no rush." Even as those words came out of her mouth, she knew she didn't mean them. She had been waiting to meeting him for weeks and now found herself a little annoyed she had more waiting. Wasn't he as excited to meet her as she was to meet him?

Catherine hung up the phone and felt letdown but told herself it probably couldn't be helped. After all he was an attorney and had been out of the country for quite some time. He was probably bogged down with a lot of work at the office. She wondered what time the antique stores closed. Maybe they stay open late on Saturday and they could still walk around a little. They were going to miss the beautiful day but that's life. These things happen. Catherine took off her dress so as not to wrinkle it and then put on her jeans. She pulled a tee shirt out of her closet and then decided not to wear it. She didn't want her hair to get messed up while pulling it over her head. Catherine decided to grab a button up the front shirt to protect her elegant and expensive hairstyle. She then retreated to the front porch swing to read a book. At least she'd get a little sunshine and enjoy the beautiful day.

James finally showed up a little before seven. Catherine was looking out of her second floor bedroom window when she saw him arrive. He pulled into her driveway behind the wheel of a red two-door convertible Jaguar, which had the top down. Catherine noticed the license tag on the Jaguar had seven letters spelling out FLAWLES.

He was an older man. Catherine guessed he was in his mid to late sixties. Since Catherine was in her late forties, there was an age gap of more years than she would have preferred. However, maybe dating someone older was the way to guarantee that she had a mature man. He was tall, big build with a little gut. Obviously he had sent her a very old picture.

When she opened the door he greeted her warmly. "How nice to finally meet you. You're just as lovely as your picture."

His comments made her smile. Catherine invited him in and asked if he would like to sit down for a minute. She had a chilled Chardonnay in the refrigerator waiting his arrival.

James agreed a glass of Chardonnay would be great to drink while they visited. He told her about his business trip and explained, "as usual," it was a success.

"What about the painting in London? Did you purchase it?"

"No. I didn't buy it after all."

"Did you get someone else to measure the wall?"

"I found out you were telling the truth about the door."

Catherine replied, "Of course I was telling the truth. What did you think, I couldn't open a door?"

"I thought maybe you just didn't want to bother helping me. I found out my workman had closed and locked the door by mistake."

James had dyed reddish brown hair that really accentuated his age. There was nothing natural looking about his hair. To Catherine, this was an indication he was probably into dating younger women. Now Catherine didn't believe every man that dyed his hair was after a young lady, but in her experience, it had been true. To her, gray hair looked so distinguished on a man. Just look at the anchormen on television and movie stars that leave their hair natural. Some of them are the classiest, sexiest men you will ever find. Look at George Clooney, Harrison Ford, Eric Braeden and James Brolin. Their gray doesn't keep them from having a distinguished handsome appearance. However, she also believed a person should do whatever makes them happy. She certainly couldn't throw any stones. She had been getting help with her, "natural" blonde hair from the salon for many years.

The other thing she noticed about his appearance was he definitely had some plastic surgery around his eyes. They looked very awake. As a matter of fact, they were so wide open she wondered if he had trouble closing them when he went to bed at night. His eyebrows were arched to a point and looked almost theatrical.

After visiting a short while, James decided it was time to head out.

While they were walking to the car, Catherine said, "I wanted to look nice for our date so I had my hair done this morning with one of the best stylists in the area."

"You look lovely. Your hair does too."

"Thanks. I was wondering, are you going to put the top up to your Jaguar?"

"The top stays down," he dictated.

Catherine immediately excused herself and turned around to go back into the house to grab a clip for her long hair. She didn't mind running around during the day with the top to a convertible down, but in the evening, on the day she just paid a fortune to get her hair done, and when they were on their way to a nice restaurant, she would have preferred to have the top up. It was a beautiful day, what was left of it, and she understood how he might not be thinking about her hair. With her hair in a clip, they headed off to Leesburg.

Catherine asked James if any of the antique shops would still be open in the evening.

"Probably not." He continued saying, "It's all junk anyway. I would never buy my antiques in those kinds of places. I only buy the finest quality antiques. Furthermore, I shop overseas because that's the only decent place to purchase antiques."

Catherine knew from that comment they would not be browsing any shops even if they were open. She was disappointed but figured she could always go on her own someday. Many of her friends had told her how great the antique shopping was in Leesburg and she trusted their judgment completely.

"Did you get a lot done at the office today?" Catherine asked.

"The office? It's Saturday. I didn't go into the office."

"I was under the impression you were late in picking me up because you had work to do."

"I didn't have office work to do. I needed to go to the grocery store and I wanted to have some light bulbs changed on one of my chandeliers at home. Besides, Miss Sunshine, Miss Poison and Miss Ivy didn't want me to leave. They missed their Daddy. I needed to spend time with them."

Now Catherine was feeling like he just told her, "I had to shampoo my hair." He could go to the store and have light bulbs changed anytime. Not to mention she was now second fiddle to three dogs. What happened to him wanting to spend more time with her?

"I have a big birthday coming up and I'm going to throw myself a party. I just haven't had the time to plan it. Money is no object. I want something very classy."

"Why don't you let me help?" she offered knowing how much fun it would be to plan a party and not have to consider money. "I'd love to plan your party. I've planned several parties in the past and have entertained a lot. I'd love to make your birthday special."

Without hesitation, James replied. "I'll pass."

"Oh. Do you want to hire a professional party planner?"

"No. It has nothing to do with that." He started laughing. In a condescending tone he said, "I know you're from Oklahoma."

"Yes?"

"Well, I don't want any type of hoe-down party. Thanks, but no thanks."

Catherine didn't know him well enough to know if he was joking or not. Did he think because she was originally from Oklahoma she was a natural born hick? For an educated man, could he be that ignorant? Surely this was his sense of humor coming out. In that case, he was sort of funny, but not that much. However, he seemed serious. She sat silent, not wanting to challenge him.

As they drove to Leesburg, they stopped for a red light on Route Seven. There was a car next to them filled with young Hispanic men. They were winking at Catherine and saying, "Baby you look so good."

Catherine laughed and told James what they were doing.

He responded, "They aren't looking at you. They're looking at the Jag. I get this all the time."

When they got to Leesburg, Catherine sat in the car until she brushed all the tangles out of her fine hair so she would be presentable at dinner. She could just imagine how tangled her hair would have been had she not had the clip holding most of it in place.

They went to a restaurant called The Lightfoot Café. James told her the restaurant was an old bank that was fully restored. It had an elegant atmosphere.

They were a little early for their reservations so their table wasn't ready yet. They went upstairs to the bar and James ordered two martinis with no olives.

"I don't really care to have a martini."

"You'll like this one," he stated.

"Really. The only thing I like about the martini is the olive. I can get that on a salad. I'd prefer to have something else to drink."

He rolled his eyes and mumbled, "I should have known. It's too sophisticated for you."

Her eyes squinted as she shot him a glaring look to show her disproval of his arrogant remark.

"One glass of champagne," he ordered without asking for her approval.

While they were at the bar he handed her a document. It had his future trips listed, stating where he would be and the dates he would be gone. He was going on business to China, London, Taiwan, Singapore, and some domestic places like New York, Las Vegas, and Dallas to name a few.

After looking at the trips, Catherine handed the list back to him telling him it was very impressive.

"Keep it," he said placing it in front of her. "Look it over and let me know which trips you want to go on."

"What? I'm not going on any trips with you. We just met."

"I figured the trip next week was too soon but you might want to consider next month's trip. It's to Paris."

"I don't even know you."

"What better way to get to know me than to go on a trip?"

"That's not the way it works with me. I need to get to know you first."

"I'm not around enough for you to get to know me. You have to go on this trip and then everything will fall into place. I'll take you to all the major sights and if you want, we can even do some shopping. I know how you women like your shopping."

Catherine gave him back the list.

James said, "I'll hang on to it for you."

When their table was ready they moved downstairs. Even though it was a Saturday night and the place was packed, the service was fantastic. James ordered a bottle of wine but Catherine told him she really didn't want to mix drinks and was a light drinker so a bottle was too much for her.

"One glass of wine would be perfect for me."

"You are being ridiculous. We'll have the bottle. Plus, bring me another martini, no olives."

When James' martini was brought to him, he took one sip and flagged his waitress down. In a rude voice he scolded, "I said no olives."

"There aren't any olives in it sir."

"Well I can tell there was an olive in it and then it was taken out. I can taste the olive juice. I can't drink this. Bring me another one and be sure no olives touch the glass. Do you understand?"

She promptly took the martini. It embarrassed Catherine the way he talked to the waitress.

A few moments later their waitress placed another drink on the table. "Wait," he demanded as he snapped his fingers at her. She obeyed and stood perfectly still waiting as he sipped the martini. "That's more like it. Thank you for finally getting it right," he said sarcastically.

Catherine knew it was going to be a long evening.

Everything on the menu looked delicious. When the waitress came over to take their order, Catherine ordered the filet mignon.

James immediately said to the waitress, "Just wait a minute. Don't write her order down yet." Looking at Catherine he continued, "They have really great fish here. Are you sure you don't want the fish?"

Catherine responded, "No, I really am in the mood for a filet mignon."

The waitress started to write the order down again but James held his hand up and scolded, "I already told you once not to write her order down. What do you think you're doing?"

"She said she wanted the filet, sir."

"I know she said that but I told you to wait. Do you understand what wait means?"

"I'm sorry sir." She stopped writing.

"Good. I'm glad you finally got it. My God, you people are frustrating. Incompetence everywhere I go," James said sarcastically. "Catherine, the fish would be a lot lighter and I know how you ladies like to watch your figures. I really think the fish would be a wiser choice for you." Looking at the waitress he said, "I'm sure you agree with me that she should order the fish."

"It's not my decision sir," the waitress politely replied.

"Well, I'm not afraid to tell it like it is. After all, there is a lot of competition in the dating world and a woman has to do everything possible to keep her figure. Especially at your age," he added while glancing at Catherine.

Catherine was livid, feeling a wave of heat rolling up her body. Before she could say anything, the waitress looked at James and declared, "She looks like a super model. What do you think I am, a fat tub of lard?"

Without backing down James responded, "Let's be honest ladies. Swimming suit season is almost upon us." Looking at Catherine he continued, "Are you sure you're ready for it? I'm just trying to help you.

I have a lot of pool parties and I don't want you to feel embarrassed. I'm only thinking of you."

All of this from an old man with dyed red hair and a big gut. If Catherine had enough money on her, and if there was a cab service in Leesburg, she would have left and taken a cab back to her house in Oakton. But as it was, she didn't know if there was a cab service in Leesburg and she did not have anywhere near the amount of money she would have needed for the substantial cab fare. It was a long way from Leesburg to Oakton in a cab, and it was going to be an even longer evening. As nice as this restaurant was, she was wishing they had eaten somewhere closer to her home so she could leave.

The waitress looked at Catherine asking her, "What will you have?"

"I'll have the filet mignon, a spinach salad, and please keep the bread coming. Oh, by the way, do you have any suggestions for dessert?"

"Yes. We have a chocolate torte to die for."

"I'd like to order that right now for later."

This pleased their waitress who by now had a big smile on her face. After all, Catherine was making a statement the waitress understood and besides, the more she ordered, the bigger the tip. It was a win/win deal for two women.

For the first time that evening, James sat silent, probably upset he had not been obeyed.

"What will you have sir?" asked the waitress.

"Caesar salad and the sea bass."

Catherine wanted to say, "Wise choice James. Swimming suit season is just around the corner," but instead, Catherine decided not to stoop to his level.

Throughout dinner James talked as if he thought everything was going great with their date. He pulled out pictures of, "my precious ladies," which were three cute little Yorkshire Terriers. Each one had a little bow in her hair.

Catherine surmised Miss Sunshine was the one with the yellow bow, Miss Ivy had the green bow and Miss Poison had the red. She was right. Just call her Sherlock! She found herself being a little jealous. After all, she wanted to be called Miss Catherine when she went to the grocery store. That would sound so much better than Ma'am. Nothing makes you feel older than to be called Ma'am. "Good day Miss Catherine," had a much better ring to it than, "Have a nice day Ma'am." Catherine was already looking over her shoulder expecting a Boy Scout to appear and help her across the street. She knew her day was coming.

Next James pulled out a picture of his, "last girlfriend." She looked to be at a maximum around twenty-four years old. She could have easily been Catherine's daughter's age. She had long blonde hair and was a striking beauty.

James told Catherine the young lady was a former model, six feet, two inches tall and was absolutely the most beautiful, sexy woman he had ever dated. He said she loved to spend the day at his pool in the nude. As a matter of fact, she usually shed her clothes when she was walking around his house. As he explained, "When you have a drop-dead gorgeous body, you don't need to cover it up with clothes."

Catherine now understood why James was wearing his business suit, but wondered if he should be wearing a trench coat and a hood over his face as well.

"She's very beautiful, but why do you feel the need to show me her picture?"

He responded, "I thought you might like to see your competition."

"I thought you said she was a former girlfriend."

"She's still around every so often. She loves to hang out at my pool. She brings her other model friends over too."

"I'm not worried about it."

"You're certainly confident."

From that response, Catherine could tell he wasn't getting the true meaning of what she was implying.

Catherine spotted the picture of Molly and her in his wallet. "Oh. I see you have our picture."

"A nice picture but I can tell you're not even wearing designer jeans."

"What?" she asked shocked.

"Your jeans, where did you get them? You shouldn't wear jeans like that. Why didn't you spend a little extra money and get some designer jeans?"

"Where do you get off talking to me that way?"

"Well, are they designer jeans or not?"

"That's beside the point. You are the rudest most arrogant man I've ever met."

"I knew it. They aren't. You could have at least bought Gucci. I own several pairs of Gucci."

"What's wrong with you? How shallow can one man be? You don't know how to be nice." Catherine could feel her temper rising. "By the way, you never thanked me for the trouble I went to when I went to your house to measure the wall and you never even thanked me for the chicken soup when you were sick."

"Well you never got into the house to measure the wall so there wasn't anything to thank you for and as far as the soup went, you gave me creamed spinach. Who in their right mind gives creamed spinach?"

"They have great creamed spinach there. Did you even try it?"

"Who am I? Popeye the Sailor Man?"

Catherine was shocked with his response and found she was beginning to despise him.

"Now grow up and drink your wine," he demanded.

"No thank you," Catherine refused. She now felt James was trying to force the wine upon her and she didn't want any wine. She wanted to keep her mind as sharp as possible around James. Besides, she told him in the first place she didn't want to share a bottle of wine. It was his own fault he ordered it and she was under no obligation to drink. Truthfully, she felt like picking up the bottle and chugging it all down to make herself numb but she decided keeping her wits about her was the best course of action for an evening with James Gordon. Besides, he would probably think they don't use wine glasses in Oklahoma. She suspected he might think she was accustomed to only drinking moonshine from the secret family distillery.

The food that night was fantastic, especially the desert. Normally Catherine wouldn't have ordered so much food but it was the principle of the thing. She didn't finish anything but ate enough to try a little of everything and she felt it made her point. And besides, the filet mignon melted in her mouth. The mashed potatoes were fantastic and the desert was well worth the calories. One of her mottoes was that it's okay to put calories in your mouth if it's really good. If the food is only so-so, it just isn't worth having to exercise it off later. This food was worth every single calorie.

As Catherine was finishing her desert, James excused himself to go to the rest room. As soon as the waitress saw him get up, she came over to the table.

"Do you need anything else?"

"No. I'm so full. Everything was marvelous! By the way, I'm so sorry about his behavior. This is our first date."

"Don't you mean your last?"

"Yes," Catherine laughed.

"I loved it when you ordered desert."

"That was funny. Plus the desert was wonderful!"

"I'm glad you enjoyed it. I hope the rest of your evening goes well."

"Thanks. It will. I'm going home."

As James and Catherine left the restaurant to head back to the car, he heard a band playing at a nightclub down the street. "Let's go check it out."

At this point, Catherine had no desire to do anything but go home. "I really don't want to, James. I need to go home."

"I like this band. I might want to hire them for my birthday party." He walked in the bar and Catherine reluctantly followed. James picked out a booth and sat down.

"I'll have a beer," he yelled to the bartender.

Catherine ordered a mineral water.

The band was great so while James talked to the band, during a break to see about hiring them, Catherine went to the ladies room. She ended up spending time talking with a group of ladies she met, which made her evening a little more pleasant.

James ended up standing at the bar, talking with the bartender. After a while, James went back to their booth so Catherine joined him, making a firm decision she was going to insist they head home.

"Did you hire them?" Catherine yelled over the band's music.

"Yes."

"Good, now let's go."

"I'm still working on my beer."

"James, I'm really tired."

"You're not tired" he exclaimed in a dismissive tone.

Catherine realized she needed another strategy. "Aren't your little darlings missing you by now? You've been traveling so much that being away tonight really isn't fair to them. We've been gone an awfully long time."

Catherine didn't know if it was the statement about his dogs or not but he pulled money from his billfold, left it on the table and scooted out of the booth. "Yes," she thought, "I'm on my way home!"

James grabbed her hand tightly and pulled her to the dance floor.

"No. I want to leave."

"Just one dance and we'll leave."

"I really need to go."

Just then the fast music stopped and the slow began.

"This is even better," he declared.

This was just Catherine's luck. James pulled her in tight to his chest and they began to dance. It was actually more like a sloppy shuffle. This man had no rhythm.

Half way through the dance he said, "You're so beautiful. I'm so glad we met." The next thing Catherine knew, James pulled her hair back and started kissing her on the neck. That was it! Catherine broke free from him, walked off the floor and headed for the door. She did not stop until she reached the Jaguar. She saw James trailing behind but at least he was coming along.

The evening had turned quite chilly. Catherine wished she had brought her wrap.

James got in the car and started the engine.

"Wait. Aren't you going to put the top up? The evening air is cold."

"No. People expect it to be down."

"What people. Nobody cares!"

"I'll turn the heater on for you." He started heading down the street with the heater going full blast. It became obvious the heater trick wasn't going to work.

"The air is cold by the time it reaches me. Please put the top up now," she yelled.

"Stop your nagging. The top stays down."

Catherine noticed a nice looking antique store on the corner. It dawned on her that the only antique she got to see on this evening was James Gordon. He was one antique she was not going to take home.

Catherine couldn't wait to be home. She started digging in her purse looking for her house keys. Even though it was a long drive back to Oakton, she wanted to have her house keys out and ready to go for a quick escape.

James drove out onto the highway but didn't go very far when he pulled the car over to the side of the road.

"What are you stopping for?" Catherine asked alarmed.

"Just be quiet and let me do the talking."

Now she noticed there were flashing lights behind them.

"Were you speeding?" Due to her obsession of finding her house keys, she had not been paying attention to his driving.

"Just be quiet," he bellowed.

An officer came up to the car. "Driver's license and registration please."

"What seems to be the problem officer?" James politely asked.

"Driver's license and registration."

"Is there a problem? I shouldn't have a tail light out. I just had my car inspected," James said as he handed the officer his documents.

The officer did not respond as he studied the license and registration.

"Nice evening. We just finished dinner and are on our way home."

"Sir, have you been drinking tonight?"

"Drinking. What would make you ask me that question?"

The officer looked very annoyed that James dodged his question.

"Sir, please step out of the car."

"Now is that really necessary?"

"Step out of the car."

James obeyed. Another police car pulled behind the other officer's car. The two officers in that car joined the first officer.

"Follow me sir," the first officer instructed James.

"What's this all about?"

"This way please," the officer directed James, who complied.

They went a short distance behind the Jag and stopped. Catherine couldn't hear everything being said but when she saw them make him walk a line and try to touch his nose, it confirmed he was stopped for drunk driving. She wondered if his car was weaving as they were going along the highway.

She started thinking about how many drinks James had consumed. There was one glass of wine at her house. She counted two martinis, one at the bar upstairs and one with dinner. He also drank wine from the bottle he had ordered with no help from her. At the nightclub she knew he ordered a beer but didn't notice if it was more than the one beer. Even so, she knew he was definitely drunk. She hadn't paid attention to the amount of alcohol he had consumed during the evening but now she was very much aware it was way too much. The funny thing was he didn't walk as if he were drunk when they left the nightclub and went back to the car. He also didn't talk like he was drunk. Maybe she was just so livid with him that she hadn't noticed. Regardless, she was beginning to think it was a blessing in disguise they got stopped. Better this than a car wreck. Looking back, she was upset with herself for not keeping better track of his drinking throughout the evening since it could have been a disaster for them or for someone else.

Once in a while Catherine could hear the officers speaking but it was hard to make out what they were saying. She did hear James saying over and over in a loud obnoxious voice, "Do you know who I am? Do you? I am an attorney at one of the most prestigious law firms in Washington, D. C." She also heard, "What will happen if I don't pass the breathalyzer?" And then he would go back to chanting, "Do you know who I am? I am an attorney at one of the most prestigious law firms in Washington, D. C."

One of the officers said, "You need to cooperate sir."

James responded, "Let my wife drive me home. That's my wife," he pointed to the car. "Let her drive me home. There's no need for any of this, my wife will take care of me."

One of the officers came to Catherine's side of the car.

"Ma'am, we're going to have to arrest your husband for DWI."

"That's not my husband. This is a very bad first date."

"I need to see your driver's license."

"My driver's license? I don't have it with me. I wasn't driving."

"You should always have your license on you, even when you aren't driving."

"I didn't know. I can give you my name and address. Would that be okay?"

"That will be fine. Name, address and your social security number, please."

Catherine quickly complied. As that officer left to verify her information, another officer approached her.

"Please step out of the car."

"Okay." Catherine obeyed. She wondered what was going to happen now? Were they going to take her in for not having her license? Surely that couldn't be against the law.

She had watched the cop shows on television and knew they couldn't be arresting her. After all, she had her shirt and shoes on. She wasn't a bad guy. She was the innocent victim of a bad date. She wondered to herself how many other women were out there having bad Saturday night dates. They might be dealing with a tightwad who wouldn't pick up the check or maybe a man who thought he had certain privileges because he did pick up the dinner bill. There were so many scenarios popping through her head. She wondered if any other women were getting pulled over by the police. Catherine had seen plenty of shows on television where couples were pulled over.

"They ain't mine. I don't know where da drugs came from. This is my cousin's car. I didn't know he had drugs under da seat," the bad date would say.

"I ain't involved in none of dis. He was just givin me a ride. I don't know dis guy," whined the slutty tattooed woman in the short torn skirt and stained halter top.

"Didn't I arrest you last month for prostitution?" stated the police officer as he gazed at the tattooed woman.

"That wurnt me. That were my twin sister."

"Your twin sister?"

"Yea. She's always gettin into trouble. I tried to steer her clear since I'm the older sister, but it's no use. She's always in trouble."

"How much older are you?" asked the officer.

"A year."

"Shut up Wanda. Just keep your trap shut. You're an idiot. You're makin it worse," said the bad date.

"Huh? Whad I do? I was just tellin him it wurnt me. It were my sister he arrested."

"Shut up! God you're stupid."

"Okay geniuses. We're taking you both in," declared the officer.

"I ain't goin back again, I just can't! Ain't no way," said the bad date.

"You should have thought of that before," the officer said as he snapped the handcuffs on the bad date. "In the car, genius. Watch your head," directs the officer as the bad date gets into the back of the squad car. "We're taking you in for possession of drugs and you," he says as he looks at Wanda, "You can call your twin sister to bail you out."

Catherine snapped out of her daydream as she heard the officer state, "You're going to have to take a breathalyzer."

"Me? Why?" Catherine asked.

"So we know you're able to drive his car home. Otherwise, we'll have to tow it."

Catherine didn't want the responsibility of driving his precious Jaguar home. What if something happened to it? "I don't want to drive his car. This Jaguar is his pride and joy. Just tow it and give me a ride to Oakton, please."

"Can't do that Ma'am. If we give you a ride, it would have to be to the station and you would have to make arrangements from there for someone to come pick you up."

It was early in the morning by now and there was no one Catherine wanted to wake up and ask to drive all the way out to Leesburg to pick her up at the police station. She agreed to take the breathalyzer test in order to get the all clear to drive his car.

She knew she had very little to drink that evening and thought she would be okay but didn't know how a breathalyzer worked and didn't know if any alcohol would still be in her system. She breathed into the breathalyzer but didn't do it hard enough the first time so the officers had her do it again. She was told she passed. As a matter of fact, it showed up zero. Catherine guessed since she had been drinking bottled water most of the evening and she had more food in her system than she usually ate in a whole weekend, she was safe.

Catherine could hear James yelling in the background. "You've got to let me talk to my wife. She has to take care of my babies."

Two officers brought James to where Catherine was standing. James looked outraged as if the officers were the bad guys. He was now handcuffed.

"You have to go by the house and take care of my babies. Promise me you'll do it. Promise me. They won't go piddle in the house and they must be walked. Otherwise they'll get an infection. Promise me you'll go by the house. Don't let them get an infection." James seemed hysterical.

"Okay, I promise."

James immediately calmed down. "This is all just terrible."

"I need your house keys," Catherine said unsympathetically.

"They're on the car key ring."

"What about your alarm system?"

"Don't worry about the alarm."

The two officers led James to their patrol car and drove off with James in the backseat. Catherine thought to herself how she never in her wildest dreams would have imagined she would see one of her dates taken away by the police. And yet she also thought it seemed very fitting for it to be James.

Catherine got into the Jag and thought about how this was going to be a great story to retell to her girlfriends. Catherine knew they would be laughing their heads off. Of course, it didn't seem to be funny at the time, but Catherine knew from experience when she and Jasmine got together, there would be humor in even the most terrible evenings.

Catherine told the remaining officer, "This Jaguar means everything to James and I really hate to drive it."

"You'll do fine," the officer encouraged her. Then he added, "You say this was your first date? Is it also your last one or are you going to let him make it up to you?"

Without hesitation she responded, "Last. Definitely the last date."

"Drive careful Ma'am."

Catherine fastened her seat belt, started the engine, turned on the headlights and headed off for home. As soon as she got going on the highway she hit the button for the top to be raised. The top didn't budge. She hit it again and it still wasn't working. Just her luck, she couldn't get the darn thing to work. She kept driving. At this point she was more concerned about getting home than getting the top up. She quickly found she had to slow down because a thick fog moved in, covering the road. She was now putting all her concentration on watching the white line on the cement, terrified she would go off the road. Suddenly a deer leaped in front of the car causing Catherine to slam on the brakes. As fast as the deer came, it was gone. Catherine's heart was racing. Luckily, she didn't hit the deer but it scared her enough that she started praying, "God, just let me get home safely and not put any scratches on James' Jag." Not that she cared about James or his Jaguar; her concern was the thought of a lawsuit from an attorney who had proven to be a jerk.

Nothing on this stretch of road looked familiar. By now there should be some form of city light. Catherine knew she couldn't have taken a wrong turn, it was a straight shot down route seven, but in her heart, she knew somehow she was lost. Of all the times to leave her cell phone at home. It was on the kitchen counter being charged and this was the first time she had ever left home without it safely in her purse.

In the distance, she could see a light. It was an all night quick stop. Yes! She could stop and ask for directions. She pulled into the quick stop and parked the car.

Catherine opened the glove box and searched for his instruction manual because she wanted to know how to put the top up on his Jag. Obviously the button wasn't working so there must be a trick she needed to figure out in order to make it function. Nothing was found in the glove box. She looked under the seats in the front and crawled to the back seat but still found nothing. Maybe the instruction manual was in the trunk. She popped the trunk open to investigate. Inside the trunk was a brief case, which Catherine clicked open and to her surprise, it was filled with hundred dollar bills. This made Catherine feel very uncomfortable. What was this? Who carries this much cash around? Her prayers started again. "Oh God please let me get home safely. Please let this nightmare end." By now all sorts of things were flashing through her head. Was this drug money? What other reason could there be for a briefcase filled with hundred dollar bills. Did he have Mafia connections? A vision of a horse's head flashed through her brain. Catherine was now thinking it was obvious she had watched too many shows on television.

It could be his emergency cash stash, or maybe he was one of those people who don't like to keep their cash in the bank, although she very seriously doubted that scenario. Whatever the reason, it was none of her business. She was no longer concerned about finding the instruction manual so she could put the top up. Catherine just wanted to go home. She closed the briefcase, shut the trunk and ran into the quick stop.

Upon entering, she saw an Asian man behind the counter. He had small round glasses, black hair with streaks of gray at his temples and a big smile.

"I'm trying to go to the Tyson Corner area and I'm lost."

"Tyson's Corner in Virginia?" he asked in choppy English.

"Yes."

"You in Maryland. You not in Virginia. You lost."

She wondered how she got to Maryland. She really was lost. James must have had the car headed in the wrong direction from the very beginning. It also didn't help that Catherine did not have a good sense of direction. There was no north, south, east or west in Catherine's world. There was only "turn left" or "turn right."

"You long way from Tyson Corner Virginia."

"Please, can you tell me how to get there?" Catherine pleaded.

"Yes, I tell you."

The man was very sweet but Catherine had a terrible time understanding him. She listened intently as he gave her directions. When she got into the car she found herself saying the directions over and over again, terrified she would forget. Usually she carried a pen and paper with her but that too was at home with her cell phone. All sorts of lessons were being learned on this date. She found the underpass and the sharp turn he had mentioned. It seemed like forever but finally she was back on route seven. "Thank you God," Catherine prayed out loud, quickly glancing upward. "Good karma to you," she wished for the Asian man who had helped her find her way. Catherine was thrilled to recognize a familiar road name. As she drove, her eyes felt so dry from the wind blowing but at this point she didn't care about the top being down, she just wanted to get home.

In the distance she heard a faint noise. Boom—boom. "What was that? Was that thunder?" she asked out loud. All of a sudden, it started pouring down rain.

"Oh, this is just great. I can't believe this is happening," she screamed. "Okay God. Are you and the angels having a good laugh? Is my Grandmother watching?" she said out loud as she chuckled. After all, she now had the best story to tell the girls. Jasmine, Katie and Miriam were going to get a real kick out of this one. Catherine couldn't believe the events of the evening. At this point her hair and dress were getting soaked. His Jaguar was getting rained in and there was nothing she could do to resolve the problem. She pressed the button again that should make the top go up but alas, it still wasn't working. Maybe that's why James didn't put the top up for her. Maybe he didn't want to tell her something was broken on his Jaguar.

As the rain poured down, there was nothing left to do but give into the moment so she broke into laughter. She knew this would be a great comedy moment on video. She broke into song. "If they could see me now, that little gang of mine."

Catherine was thankful the rain quit as quickly as it had started. The turnoff for James' house was coming up and she thought about the promise she had made to him earlier about stopping to walk his little darlings. She knew at the time she made the promise she had no intention of following through. She only agreed to walk his dogs so he would calm down. However, she was now having second thoughts. She started thinking about those little dogs and how James said they would get an infection if she didn't take them out. It wasn't their fault he was incarcerated. She shouldn't take it out on them because James was a big jerk.

Catherine thought of her sister Rita and her sweet dog Abby. Rita loved that dog as if it were her own child. Once Catherine thought of Abby, she knew what she had to do. She was going to go by his house and walk his three dogs. Sometimes she hated that she was a kind person. Catherine found the turnoff and headed towards James' house.

After carefully maneuvering the car down the dark and windy road, she reached his house. As soon as she shut the engine off, she could hear the dogs yapping inside. She ran to the front door, quickly opening and closing the door so the dogs wouldn't escape.

All three dogs were yapping continuously. She wanted to find their leashes so she wouldn't have to worry about them getting away. She glanced around but saw nothing and was too impatient to search in any length. She just wanted to get this over with and go home.

As Catherine quickly looked around, she gasped and stumbled back. She caught a glimpse of herself in the entryway mirror and it was frightening. Her hair was frizzy, her dress was stuck to her body and her eyes were bloodshot from her contact lenses being irritated from the wind due to driving with the top down. In addition to all that, she had black mascara dripping down her cheeks. She remembered how proud she was with the way she looked earlier and knew the pride was now gone. There was no evidence of an expensive hairstyle. There was nothing of beauty in the mirror. She didn't recognize the woman she saw, but the funny thing was, she didn't care. Catherine just wanted to go home.

Catherine did realize some good news; the dogs were doing a lot of high-pitched yapping but no biting. So far, so good. She couldn't find any leashes and wasn't sure what their reaction would be if she tried to pick them up so she grabbed two of them by the top of their collar and walked hunched over to the front door. She quickly let go of one dog to reach for the doorknob. To her surprise, the dog stayed in place. She kept the other dog back with one foot, grabbed the one dog's collar again and guided them both outside. Once again she quickly released one dogs collar to close the door behind her.

As Catherine walked off the stone path, onto the grass, her heels sunk into the soggy rain soaked ground, making it difficult to walk. She took the two dogs to a nearby bush, hoping they would do their thing. To her surprise, they both quickly urinated. As she was walking hunched over, back to the house, Catherine could hear the phone ringing. She wondered who would be calling James at this early hour of the morning. By the time she got back into the house, the phone had stopped ringing. The dogs were settling down and not yapping. As she grabbed the third dog by her collar and walked stooped over to the front door, she could hear a beeping noise.

"Is that an alarm?" she said out loud. "It couldn't be. James said not to worry about the alarm."

She took the third dog, which she knew to be Miss Sunshine from the yellow bow in her hair, to the good luck bush. Just as they reached the bush, an ear piercing house alarm went off. It scared Miss Sunshine into urinating right away. It scared Catherine so much she was thankful she didn't join her. At that moment, Catherine lost her balance and fell into a puddle of mud, still holding tight to Miss Sunshine's collar. It took Catherine a moment to regain her composure. She looked at her beautiful black dress now covered in mud. She was really not having a good evening. Poor little Miss Sunshine was terrified. The house alarm had scared Miss Sunshine and now Catherine's fall had startled her even more. Catherine slowly pushed herself up from the ground as far as she could, while still holding onto Miss Sunshine's collar. As she took her first step, one of her shoes stayed behind in the mud. Catherine picked it up and held it under her arm. Hunched over and walking lopsided from the lack of one shoe, Catherine led Miss Sunshine back into the house.

The alarm was so loud she was sure anyone within a three-mile radius could hear the intense screeching noise. Miss Sunshine, Miss Poison and Miss Ivy were yapping even louder now. They did not like this loud ear piercing alarm anymore than Catherine. That was not her problem. She had done her good deed.

Catherine hated the fact she was going to have to drive the Jaguar home but she had no choice. She wanted out of there quickly. As she closed the door, being very careful not to let the dogs out, she wondered if she was getting permanent ear damage from the noise of the alarm. Never in her life had she heard anything so loud. She wondered why the neighbors hadn't come running to check out the commotion. She guessed since James had so much property, the nearest neighbor wasn't as bothered as she was with the roaring alarm. Catherine was going to be very glad to be moving away from the extremely loud sound and heading home because she really couldn't stand another second of that alarm. She slammed the door shut, happy to muffle a bit of the noise.

Suddenly, a voice startled her. "Don't move. Put your hands on your head." The voice was coming from directly behind her. She quickly started to turn around.

"Don't move," he screamed.

There were four patrol cars with eight officers. From her peripheral vision it looked as if one of the officers had his gun pointed towards her. She could see the reflection of flashing lights in the front door windowpane.

"You don't understand," she yelled, trying to explain over her shoulder as she attempted to turn towards the officers.

"Stop where you are! Don't take another step. Put your hands on your head."

Catherine realized she'd better do what she was told. She also realized she probably looked like some drug addict prostitute. Frizzy hair, blood shot eyes, wet muddy dress clinging to her body, and black mascara down her cheeks. This situation wasn't looking good.

Three of the officers went into the house and the others stayed out with Catherine. In a few minutes, the alarm stopped. The officers led Catherine inside and asked her to explain what she was doing inside his house. She explained that James had asked her to walk his dogs for him.

"At three-thirty in the morning?"

"Wow. I knew it was late but I didn't know it was that late. We were out and he got detained and asked me to walk his dogs." She wasn't sure at this point if it would be to her benefit to tell the officers that James had been arrested.

"You mean he asked you to walk his dogs but he didn't give you the code to his alarm?"

"Yes. He led me to believe it was off." The officers glanced at each other. She knew they didn't believe her.

"Why didn't you pick up the phone when the alarm company called?"

"Oh, was that them? I was in the bushes with the dogs. Wait. I clearly could have stated that better. Although actually, I really was in the bushes, or beside the bushes with the dogs," she nervously babbled.

"In the bushes with the dogs?"

"Yes," she said.

"Go on. I'd like to hear this story."

"Please, let me explain. I couldn't find the leashes so I had to take two out. Of course that was Miss Poison and Miss Ivy because they do everything together so I figured they would probably urinate together and then I took the other one, Miss Sunshine. I knew it was her because of the yellow bow and they were all yapping so loud at first that I didn't hear the beeping noise or else I would have known it was the alarm company on the phone and I would have had a warning you were coming." Oh no. That didn't sound right. She could hear the panic in her voice. She was in hyper babble mode. When she is really nervous, she talks too fast, doesn't always make sense and babbles. She was definitely in hyper babble mode. She wasn't sure even she believed her story. This wasn't good. She knew if she stayed in hyper babble mode, they would think she was on speed. She had to slow down and start making sense if she wanted the officers to believe her. To keep from making things worse, she decided to tell the officers the truth from the beginning, if they would listen.

"James is in jail," she quickly blurted out. "If you'd just let me explain everything." She was still talking too fast.

One of the officers told Catherine to slow down, take some deep breaths and start from the beginning. Catherine began to explain all the events of the evening as best she could from the beginning of her date, emphasizing it was a first date, to his rude behavior, to his being stopped by the police for DWI, to his yelling, "I am an attorney at one of the most prestigious law firms," to his arrest, to his plea for his dogs, to her being forced to drive the Jaguar, to the fog, the deer, her getting lost, the rain with the top down to the Jaguar and up to where she was now; standing there surrounded by policemen.

Listening to herself tell the story, she started visualizing herself behind bars. It was all too far fetched for anyone to believe. She could just see her mug shot with frizzy hair, an unkempt appearance, and a frazzled expression on her face. Of course that would be the picture the photographers would use in the newspaper and on the television news. Her old high school sweetheart, whom she hadn't seen in years, would see her photograph on the front page of the paper with the headline reading *Police Catch Great Falls Robber*. Of course, her old boyfriend would be thanking God they never got together and he would be talking to everyone about how she really let herself go over the years, probably due to the drugs and the sordid path she had chosen in life.

Catherine now envisioned herself being taken away in handcuffs, all along yelling, "I'm innocent I tell you, innocent." Of course she would sound like every other suspected criminal who was brought into the police department.

The press would be camped out in front of her parent's home, waiting for an interview.

"I just don't know what went wrong. I was a good mom," sobbed her mother. "In no way should this reflect upon me."

Her father of course would be shaking his head saying, "I know she's innocent, she would never steal. She's such a good sweet daughter."

"That's not entirely true," her mother explained. "Remember in second grade when she was caught stealing a cookie from the cafeteria? She must not have learned her lesson."

"You mean to tell me your daughter has stolen in the past?" the journalist would ask.

"It was only once," her father defended her, "And it was a chocolate chip cookie. They were her favorite."

"I knew we should have grounded her for more than two days. We were too lenient," her mother chimed in. "Of all my children, I always knew she would be the one to get into trouble."

The journalist would then look into the camera and say, "You heard it here on NBC, the station that finds the truth, no matter how painful. From chocolate chip cookies to breaking and entering, it's a sad tale that we've heard before. Why did Catherine, who was raised in a caring, loving family, decide to choose a life of crime? We may never know."

Catherine had now snapped out of her daydream. She looked at the officers surrounding her who said nothing about her story. She wondered what was going to happen next. Would the word incarcerated be in her vocabulary when talking about her life?

One of the officers left the house while the others stood there looking at her in amazement. She was sure they thought she was a nut case.

A few minutes later, the officer returned with a big smile on his face. "You've had quite an evening. I just called the Leesburg police department and your story checks out. You say this was your first date with this guy?"

"Yes," she said relieved he had confirmed her story.

All the officers started laughing. Catherine found herself joining them.

"You mean to tell me you drove his Jag in the rain with the top down?" asked one of the officers.

"I didn't have a choice, the button didn't work."

"The button didn't work," repeated an officer.

They laughed even harder. "This is great. A hot shot attorney gets his just rewards," one of the officers said with delight.

Another officer chimed in, "Look at this place, I'm doing something wrong with my life. Can you imagine living in a place like this?"

For the first time Catherine looked at her surroundings. His house was extraordinary, something right out of *Architectural Digest*. The house was furnished with formal antiques. The floor to the living room was marble, with oriental rugs placed throughout. Elegant French tables stood beside a richly colored red and gold antique sofa. In the center of the room hung a magnificent crystal chandelier. There was an oversized marble fireplace with columns along the far wall. Two high back chairs adorned each side of the fireplace. Above the fireplace hung one large oil painting of Miss Sunshine, Miss Poison and Miss Ivy. As Catherine looked around the room, the only word she could think of was, "Wow."

"What a life this man leads," one officer observed.

"My wife would love this place. We could fit our house in his living room alone," another officer responded.

One of the officers looked at Catherine and said, "I bet you're ready to get home."

"I sure am."

"Let's get you out of here."

As Catherine walked outside, she locked the house and followed two of the officers to their patrol car.

"Can you give me a ride home? I live in Oakton."

"Afraid not. Just drive his Jag home. The rain has stopped."

"I really don't want to drive his car anymore. Could I please have a ride?"

"Sorry, we can't give rides. Just drive his car. It'll be okay."

Catherine found herself getting back into the Jaguar once more. This also meant her contact with James wasn't over. She now had possession of his car.

The drive home seemed to take forever. She kept thinking about taking a quick shower, putting on dry nightclothes and climbing into bed between nice clean sheets. That would be a wonderful feeling.

When Catherine pulled in her driveway, her daughter Molly came running out. "Where have you been? It's five-thirty in the morning. A simple phone call would have done."

Catherine knew where Molly had gotten that speech.

"I know, I'm so sorry. You won't believe the evening I've had."

Suddenly Molly became aware her mother had just stepped out of a Jaguar.

"More importantly, why are you driving a Jaguar and when can I borrow it?"

They both started laughing. Molly already knew the answer to the second part of her question.

As they went inside the house, Catherine started quickly explaining a little about the evening, not getting into the details because she was so tired and wanted to go to bed. Satisfied enough for five-thirty in the morning, Molly went to bed.

Catherine went to the linen closet and grabbed all her towels and went out to the car to dry it down. She was surprised it wasn't more soaked. After she felt she'd done a pretty good job of drying out the inside of his car, she came inside and started getting ready for bed. She quickly shed her wet muddy clothes and stepped into the shower. The warm water felt great. If she hadn't been so tired, she could have stood there for an hour, getting the chill off her bones. But as it was, she was too exhausted to enjoy the luxury of a long shower.

As she crawled into bed and pulled the sheet over her, she heard the sound of thunder in the distance. "Give me a break," she said as she looked up, knowing someone up there was having a blast watching her tonight. Or the way things were going, maybe someone from below was having some fun at her expense.

She realized James' car needed to be protected from any further rain. She crawled out of bed, slipping on some house shoes and heading for the hall closet. Catherine had just bought a new shower curtain. She opened the package and went outside to cover the top of the Jag to protect it from any more rain. After that, she went back to bed.

Just then Molly entered and informed her there was a saved message. She had let it go to voice mail because she thought it was a wrong number since it showed up as Loudoun County Jail on the Caller ID. Now Molly figured it wasn't a wrong number but was probably James.

Catherine retrieved the message and heard James say, "I know you set off the alarm at the house but don't worry about that. The main thing is that you took care of my ladies and the car."

Catherine thought he sounded like a pimp.

"Also, I can't let anyone at the firm know I'm here so you'll have to bail me out. I'll give you a number to call so you'll know what time you need to be here. I'm counting on you. You're my only phone call so you've got to come through for me. No one in the firm can know." He then gave her a phone number and instructed her to call around ten o'clock that morning.

Catherine couldn't believe the nerve of this guy. He must know other people. She decided right then and there she was not going to bail him out. She was so livid with him. She was worried she wouldn't be able to calm down and go to sleep. That was the last thought she had before passing out.

Usually Catherine and Molly would go to eight-thirty mass or at the latest, ten o'clock mass, but since they had both been up all night, they felt no guilt in skipping church. Catherine woke up around ten thirty and Molly was still sound asleep. Catherine looked out the bedroom window to check on the Jag. Sure enough, there it was, still covered with her new shower curtain. Luckily, it had not rained anymore.

Catherine thought about James and her being his one phone call. She called the number he left for her and asked the officer who answered the phone if he could give James one more phone call or find out from him the name of one of his other friends because she didn't want to be involved anymore. The officer told Catherine it was not possible and she should call back around two o'clock to check on his status.

If only Ellen, who had fixed her up on this date in the first place, and her husband Martin were still in town, she would have let Martin handle it, but they were in Chicago by now. Catherine called the law firm where James worked, deciding she had no loyalty to this man and wanted to pass him off to someone else. She didn't care if he didn't want anyone to know at the firm. She didn't want to be inconvenienced anymore. However, to her disappointment, the phone at the firm just rang and rang. No one at the firm was working or picking up the phone on a Sunday.

In the meantime, Catherine's next door neighbor's little boy was outside shooting with his BB gun at cans lined up on his fence. A few weeks before, he had shot the tail light to her car out, leaving her a broken light to repair. All of a sudden Catherine had a vision of him shooting at the Jaguar. Now she knew she shouldn't care since it wasn't her Jag, but the truth was she didn't want the hassle of anything happening to that car while it was in her possession.

At two o'clock she reluctantly called the number James had left on her voice mail. The officer told her she could come anytime to pick up James since he had already been to court. As much as Catherine hated to, she decided to drive to Leesburg so all of this would be behind her. She would get James out, have him drop her off at her house, and that would be the end of him. The thought of him driving away from her home with his Jaguar pleased her, and the sooner the better.

Catherine went into Molly's room and gently woke her. "I'm leaving to go bail James out of jail."

Molly replied, "These are not words I want to hear from my mother's mouth."

Catherine drove to Leesburg with a map in the car and her cell phone in her purse. Even though it was a cloudy day, she was thankful it was not raining. When she entered the jailhouse, James was standing there in a bright orange jumpsuit. His wrists were in handcuffs and his legs were shackled. His dyed hair was smashed against his head on one side with a large cowlick in the back. The color of his hair looked as bright as the orange jumpsuit he was wearing.

When James saw Catherine, he took a few short wobbly steps and said, "Baby, it's so good to see you."

"Don't baby me. What's left to do so you can leave?"

The officers handed James his clothes and directed him to another room.

Catherine watched James wobbling away. She asked the officers why James had his legs shackled.

A prisoner ran away once so now everyone has to wear shackles.

A few moments later James appeared. He said he had already paid his own bail and was free to leave.

Catherine and James went out to his Jaguar and he opened the door to the passenger side, but before Catherine could get in, he plopped himself down.

"What are you doing?"

"They took my drivers license away from me."

"Oh great, now I have to drive."

"What are you talking about? Nobody says they have to drive a Jaguar. I would think it would be a privilege for you."

"A privilege to drive you around?"

"I can see you're really in a bad mood today."

Catherine started the engine but before she pulled out, she told James she wanted the top to the Jag put up. He immediately complied by pushing the same button she had pushed all night long only this time it worked.

"I tried that last night while I was driving back and couldn't get the top to go up."

"You tried it while you were driving?"

Catherine didn't respond. Now she knew it was a simple procedure. The car should be stopped. A simple solution she wished she had learned the previous night.

When they were about a block away from the courthouse, James informed her he had made friends with one of the guys in jail. James said the guy could get out of jail if someone would stand in front of the judge and tell the judge that he was an okay guy.

"Are you interested?" he asked.

"Are you kidding me? What's wrong with you? Why would I do something like that?"

There was silence for a while, but not long enough.

"It was terrible in there Catherine. They stripped me down and sprayed me, then threw me in a room with about thirteen drunks. It was the worst night of my life."

"Don't talk to me about a bad night. I didn't get home until five-thirty in the morning."

Catherine waited for him to ask her why but he didn't.

He continued, "My breakfast was terrible but the guys told me to eat it anyway because it would help get the alcohol through my system so I could leave sooner."

Catherine wondered if the guys just wanted to be away from him as quickly as possible.

"There was no privacy for going to the rest room. Everything was right out in the open. It was terrible, just terrible. You can't imagine what they've put me through. I had no way to brush my teeth. No privacy, no conveniences, nothing! It was deplorable! I tell you, I didn't deserve that kind of treatment."

Catherine had no response. She just wanted to get home.

"I had one break. I had a female judge. I've always had a way with the ladies and I could tell she liked me and knew I was a step above the rest. I could tell she realized I didn't belong there with the other criminals. Those guys were deadbeats. I'm of a different caliber. She could tell. She knew. I could see it in her eyes."

"Criminals? Just a moment ago you wanted me to go before the judge as a character reference for one of those guys and say he was okay."

"Don't worry about that now. I can tell you're in a bad mood. I know it's not your time of the month. You're too old for that."

Catherine visualized flooring the gas pedal and heading straight for a cliff. Of course she would jump out at the last moment, rolling on the ground to safety, leaving him flying with his Jaguar into space. She could hear him yelling, "You can't do this to me. I'm with one of the most prestigious law firms in Washington, D.C." His voice would be fading as he flew further away. She snapped out of her daydream. A smile came to her face.

As they got closer to his house, James blurted out, "You'll need to stop somewhere so I can get a cappuccino and something decent to eat."

"I can't. I've got to get home to Molly."

"It won't take that long," James continued. "Catherine, I don't think you understand how bad the food was in there. I really need to eat some good food and I'm not sure what I have at home. Besides, I'm too exhausted to fix anything for myself."

Catherine wondered if he was now going to ask her to cook him a meal but luckily he didn't go down that road.

"How are my little darlings?"

"Fine," Catherine replied.

"They got to relieve themselves outside right."

"Yes, James," she responded with a sigh.

"Thank God. I recently purchased a new custom made rug that I had shipped from China and I didn't want to take a chance of them urinating on it."

Catherine was now livid and gave him a dirty look. She should have known it wasn't about the dogs getting an infection. It was just one more example of the same selfish behavior on his part.

There was more silence until they reached his driveway. Then he said, "I want you to know you've made major brownie points with me."

This proved to Catherine that this man was totally clueless. Where did he get off talking about how she made major brownie points with him! Who cares! It didn't matter. It amazed Catherine how an obviously successful attorney could be so dense.

"You can come inside and use the phone if you need someone to pick you up."

"I don't want to impose on anyone. You're calling a cab to take me home and you are going to give me the money to pay for it."

"I don't have any cash with me. All I've got is this ten dollar bill," he said as he pulled the ten out of his wallet.

Catherine knew he had a briefcase of cash in the trunk of the Jag but decided it might be best not to mention the cash. She didn't want him to know she had been in the trunk of his car and felt it was best he not know she had knowledge of any money. She took the ten dollars and waited out front for the cab. It cost her forty dollars plus a tip to get from his house to hers and she was upset to be out the cash. Even though she was irritated with being out the money, she was still thankful the nightmare of a date was over once and for all.

Two days later the florist delivered a bouquet of roses to her doorstep. The note said, "Looking forward to seeing you again." Catherine was getting ready to throw them in the trash when she changed her mind. She drove with the flowers to a retirement home down the street from her house. She was happy to turn the negative roses into a positive. She did not call to thank him for the roses.

Three days later James called Catherine. She was expecting this call. After all, it was finally time for her to receive a much-deserved apology for his behavior and a thank you for everything she had done for him. Of course, she had no intention of ever going out with him again, but that was beside the point. A little groveling on his part would be just fine.

"Catherine did you hit anything with my Jaguar?"

"No, I was very careful with your car."

"Well, all I know is that the front wheel alignment was fine when we drove to Leesburg and now it's off. I have to have someone take the car into the shop because it's messed up."

Furious, Catherine hung up the phone without saying another word to James. Catherine realized that to expect an apology or any groveling on his part was giving him way too much credit. A man like James could not see beyond his next expectation.

You may think this is where it ends, but no. One week later Catherine received a message on her answering machine from an attorney representing James.

"I need you to call me so we can discuss what happened to you and James."

Catherine wanted nothing to do with James or his attorney so she did not respond.

A few days later she received a big package in the mail. James sent her a stack of papers about an inch thick, all to do with him. On the top of the documents was another large photo of James. His resume was next and then there were articles about James working with one of the Presidents of the United States, a list of books he had written, and all his career accomplishments. There was a note attached saying, "I thought this would help you get to know me better and help our case in court."

Catherine threw the papers away.

The next day at work, her phone rang. It was James's attorney saying he needed to discuss the harassment the Leesburg policemen had given to her and James.

"I wasn't harassed by the police," Catherine responded.

"I'd like for us to meet in my office so I can help you recall the events that took place the evening of James' terrible ordeal."

"I wasn't aware you were there? I think what you are really asking me to do is to go to court and perjure myself for the sake of your lying client. I do recall James being a drunken jerk to me, to the waitress, and to the officers. If you subpoena me, you should consider me to be a hostile witness. Please don't harass me at my job or my home anymore." Catherine quickly hung up the phone.

A minute later the phone rang. It was his attorney again. "We aren't going to need you in court after all."

Catherine heard from Ellen a month later. Ellen said James told her husband Martin it had not work out between himself and Catherine because he was looking for a lady who wouldn't be intimidated to travel with him and he felt since Catherine was from Oklahoma, she was uncomfortable traveling. Ellen said she knew something was up with that story and wanted to know what happened. Ellen also said James had explained to Martin he and Catherine were just too different. He was right.

Catherine updated Ellen on her experiences with James on the night of their date.

Martin called Catherine later that day and jokingly asked if she could help Ellen and him put on a hoedown for Ellen's next birthday party. Yee-haw. He also said he would love for her and Molly to come visit, if they weren't too intimidated to travel to Chicago. He teased Catherine by telling her that instead of riding the tractor to Chicago, there was something called, "a jet."

Catherine laughs when she thinks back to the first time she saw the red Jaguar with the license tag that read FLAWLES. She can think of a lot more appropriate license tags for James.

YOU BUG ME

When Katie's daughter Samantha was very young, Katie would use a simple formula to decide if the man was worth a date. She would ask herself if this man was worth going out with while she paid a baby-sitter to watch her daughter. Katie just didn't have money to spare so this formula worked out great. Most of the time, she did not go on a second date. However, a co-worker fixed her up with a man named Bob who she described as a nice, quiet man. Katie hoped he would be worth paying the baby-sitter for her first date and if all went well, a second date.

On the evening of her date, she curled her short blonde hair and left some of the hair in ringlets for a tousled appearance. Katie put on a simple black dress and wore her only good piece of jewelry, her pearls. She was really looking forward to getting out of the house and having some adult conversation, as opposed to an evening of reading Dr. Seuss and oohing over the latest drawing with crayon. Bob told Katie he had made reservations at a really nice restaurant in Georgetown so Katie was anticipating a wonderful evening out. Katie took Samantha to the baby-sitter's house and hurried back home to wait for Bob.

Bob showed up a little early, but Katie didn't mind. She was ready to go plus she was already paying the sitter so it was better they got an early start. Bob announced the dinner reservations weren't for another hour so they should not leave yet.

While Katie fixed them both a drink, Bob went to the living room to wait. When Katie appeared with the drinks, she was surprised to see Bob had made himself very much at home. He had kicked off his shoes, exposing his green socks, and was stretched out on the sofa. He said it was an exceptionally comfortable sofa and Katie agreed. Before she bought the sofa, she had tested it herself to be sure it was not only beautiful, but also long enough to spread her body out and take restful naps.

As she handed Bob his drink she expected him to sit up. He stayed stretched out and adjusted two throw pillows that were propping his head up, which made it easier to sip his beverage. Only instead of sipping, he quickly gulped his drink until it disappeared.

Placing the glass on the floor he said, "You can take it to the kitchen later."

Even though Katie thought he was rude, she kept silent.

"So, you probably want to know all about me," Bob said. "I used to run my own business. I guess you could say I was the CEO. I had a partner but he didn't know anything about business. It was left to me to make all the client appointments, run the financial part and basically do everything."

As he spoke, he positioned his hands in a praying position. Katie wondered if he was going to break into a prayer over his business.

"How did the two of you get started working together?" she asked.

"That's not important right now. The point I'm trying to make is that I carried the load. I was the one with all the knowledge."

"What kind of business was it?"

"Development of a new software."

"What kind?"

"It's a little too complicated to explain to you right now."

"Give me a try. You don't know this but in the past, I ran my own business too. It was just for a short while but I learned a lot. We might have a few similar experiences."

"That's not what I want to concentrate on right now. Now where was I? Oh yes. So, I do the best I can to teach him how things should be done."

He continued to hold his hands as if in prayer, occasionally wringing them and then bringing them back to a praying position. He was beginning to remind Katie of a praying mantis. She wondered if his green socks would soon turn brown to match the color of her sofa.

"So what happened that made your business fail?"

"You need to pay attention. That's what I've been saying. My partner didn't know anything. He made it fail. Now please, let me proceed. I hate interruptions."

Katie found herself very annoyed. Since when did showing interest, or at least faking interest, become an interruption? His voice faded as she began to daydream. She wondered how long she would have to listen to his rambling. He didn't want any participation on her part. He just wanted to talk and have her be silent. She began to realize why the female praying mantis eats her mate. You can't argue with nature.

"Oh, I hate it when that happens!" Bob exclaimed.

"What?" Katie asked as she snapped out of her trance.

"I forgot what I was talking about."

"A praying mantis."

What?"

"I mean, shouldn't we be going?"

"We're okay," he responded dismissively.

As he rambled on about himself and his past financial problems, Katie felt as if she were a psychiatrist and should be charging him money for a psychiatric session. Not once did he stop to ask Katie about herself, her job, or her family. As a matter of fact, Katie didn't think it really mattered if it was her sitting there or not. Bob would have talked to anyone who would listen. She was merely providing the sofa and being a sounding board. He had no intention of getting to know anything about her or for that matter, even engaging her in any conversation.

At the conclusion of one of his failed business stories, Katie rose from her chair and noted to Bob they needed to be leaving if they were going to make their dinner reservations on time. She reminded him how traffic could also be a factor.

Just then, a spider came down on a spun thread of silk from the ceiling, right in front of Katie. She screamed as she jumped back to avoid contact. She ran to the library shelf and grabbed an old encyclopedia and quickly dropped it in order to smash the spider that was now on the carpet. The spider jumped so Katie screamed again.

At the same time, Bob realized what was going on and yelled, "Stop! Stop! What are you doing?"

"Spider!"

As Katie reached for the encyclopedia to attempt another smash hit, Bob grabbed it from her. "Let me handle this," Bob said as he took the encyclopedia from Katie. Bob put the encyclopedia on the coffee table, took his empty glass and quickly placed it over the spider.

"Good thinking! Now it won't get away," Katie said.

"Do you have any cardboard or a piece of paper?"

"Cardboard or paper? What do you need cardboard for?"

"You'll see."

Katie ran to the other room and quickly returned with a piece of thin cardboard. Bob gently slid the cardboard under the glass. Then he carefully got up and slowly walked to the front door. He instructed Katie to open the door.

"Aren't you going to kill it?"

"Just open the door," he commanded.

Katie obeyed as Bob placed the cardboard on the ground and lifted the glass.

"You're free now. Go, go, you're free. No one meant you any harm. Go now and be with your own kind."

Katie wondered at that moment what was Bob's kind.

"What did you do that for? I hate spiders. Now it'll just find its way back into the house."

"You're wrong to want to kill the spider. You're taking away a life. You have no right to play God and that is exactly what you're doing when you take the life of one of His creature. You should never kill any creatures of God."

"Are you serious?" Katie asked, astonished. Suddenly she started smiling as she had her own secret joke, thinking about a spider eating a praying mantis.

"Yes I'm serious. Why do you feel you have the right to kill? You should be ashamed of yourself," he scolded.

"It was just a spider. They bite you know."

"It wasn't just a spider. It was a living creature."

"I've heard about reincarnation with cows but never spiders. Was it a relative?" she said trying to make light of the situation.

Bob frowned.

As Katie stood in the doorway with the front door open, a fly flew in her house. "How do you feel about flies?"

Bob walked into the house without responding. Katie guessed she should wait until later to get the evil ceremonial fly swatter out from under her kitchen sink.

Katie expected Bob to start putting his shoes on but instead he stretched back out on the sofa.

"This sofa is really comfortable."

"I know."

"I could lay here and talk all night."

Katie did not want to sit there any longer. She did not get all dressed up and take Samantha to the sitters, just to sit in her own living room.

"Look Bob, if we're going to make it to dinner, we really need to get going." As she spoke, she noticed for the first time that Bob was very hairy. He had thick black hair all over the back of his hand. His hair was even sticking out from his shirt collar and going up the side of his neck. Maybe he was a relative to a spider, or it could be the fly? There were so many bugs to choose from and she was sure he was somehow related. At that moment, she chuckled to herself. She thought of the perfect name for Bob. Bob the bug.

"I think we should just stay here. I haven't felt this relaxed in ages, and besides, I'm really enjoying talking with you. Plus," he continued, "I'm not hungry."

The next thing Katie knew, Bob had started another story. She politely interrupted him and announced, "If we aren't going to go out, I need to pick my daughter Samantha up at the baby-sitters."

"Who?"

"My daughter Samantha."

"You have a kid?"

"Yes."

"I didn't know that. You never mentioned it."

"Really, I need to get Samantha now."

"Oh, alright. Go ahead and I'll wait here. I'm just too comfortable to move. Go on, I'll be fine."

Katie couldn't believe this guy.

"I'm really not comfortable with you staying here while I'm gone."

"It's not a problem. Really, I don't mind," Bob responded.

"But I do."

"Get over it," was his reply.

Katie got up and went to the entryway. As she opened the front door she screamed, "A spider, a spider. Bob, come quick."

Bob leaped up and ran to Katie's rescue, or maybe it was to the spider's rescue. "Where?" he asked.

"Right there," she pointed outside.

"Just leave it alone. It won't hurt anything. It's outside."

"No. It'll come back in the house. I need it further away from the house. Will you capture it and put it away from my front door?"

"It'll be fine."

"Please Bob. I need you to move it."

"You're being ridiculous."

"If you don't do something, I'm going to have to get the Raid."

"Okay, okay. Where is it?"

"Over there," she pointed.

"I don't see it."

"Step outside, it's hard to see from here."

When Bob stepped outside, Katie yelled, "Stay there, I'll get the glass and cardboard."

Katie ran into the living room, grabbed Bob's shoes, ran back to the front door and tossed the shoes outside, slamming and locking the door.

She stood there for a moment in silence, not believing what she had just done. Her heart was pounding.

Bob turned the doorknob, trying it several times. "Katie, you locked the door."

Katie stood still with her ear to the door.

"Katie, did you hear me? You locked the door on me. Open up."

He rang the doorbell several times in a row.

Katie didn't move a muscle. She still couldn't believe what she had done. Would it have been kinder to just spray him with Raid and let him join his relatives?

When Katie didn't answer, she heard him say, "It's okay, there's no spider here. You can open the door."

Katie stood in silence.

Bob rang the doorbell again.

Katie didn't move.

After a minute, she heard Bob say, "Katie, Katie, are you there? What's going on? If you don't open the door then we won't be going to dinner."

Katie stood with her ear pressed to the door, wondering how much longer it would take before Bob would give up and go away.

"I guess I'll go. I'll call you later."

She stood frozen at the door until she finally heard his car door slam shut and him drive away. She knew she made the right decision. It would never have worked out with Bob because he really bugged her.

THE SEATING CHART

After mass on Sunday, Catherine and her daughter, Molly, would usually go to the church lobby to visit with some of their friends. One Sunday a man came up to Catherine and introduced himself as Jay. He had a nice smile and seemed pleasant. Jay had thick wavy black hair, olive skin and the longest black eyelashes, which made his big brown eyes gorgeous. They visited for a couple of Sundays in a row after mass. Through the course of their talking, they discovered they lived just a few blocks from each other.

One Sunday it was an absolutely beautiful day. Jay asked Catherine if she and Molly would like to come back to his house, sit on his deck and have a glass of iced tea. He had two daughters that were a little older than Molly and they were with him that weekend. His daughters did not attend mass because their mother sent them to a different church, however, they would be at his house waiting for him to return. Molly already had plans for the day but Catherine was available. After mass Catherine dropped Molly off at her girlfriend's house and then proceeded home to change out of her church dress. She put on some navy blue shorts with a crisp white cotton top and headed for Jay's place.

Jay's property was at the end of a dead end dirt road. As Catherine drove closer to his house, she could see several junk cars on cement blocks in the yard. The grass was overgrown and weeds were everywhere. The house was a small bungalow with white peeling paint and a rain gutter hanging loose from the roof.

His daughters were outside washing the car, which was parked on the side of the yard. The minute they saw Catherine drive up, they stopped what they were doing and came over to greet her. They were very polite, cute girls with outgoing personalities. They walked Catherine to the side deck, where their father was waiting.

Jay had changed into shorts, a shirt and was barefoot. He had a pitcher of tea, two glasses and a bucket of ice ready on the deck table.

"Welcome," Jay warmly greeted her.

"Get back to washing the car girls." His daughters obeyed.

"Watch your step Catherine, the deck steps need repairing. I've been so busy working on my cars that I just haven't had time to take care of everything around the house."

As Catherine carefully maneuvered up the fragile wooden steps to the deck, Jay reached his hand in the ice bucket to retrieve ice for their tea.

The sun felt great and there was just enough of a breeze that it was a perfect day for sitting outside. As they sat there sipping their tea, Jay began picking the dirt out from under his toenails. A moment later, he reached in the ice bucket with his hand and threw a couple of additional ice cubes in his drink.

"Do you want a little more ice? I was too stingy the first time around."

"No, I'm fine," Catherine quickly responded as she placed her hand over her glass. At the same time she noticed the chair she was sitting in was filthy and the dirt was already on her white top.

As they sat there visiting, Catherine enjoyed the sound of the birds chirping in his yard. The yard may have looked atrocious but it seemed to be a great haven for birds. Unfortunately, the nice conversation and the quiet time listening to the birds was short lived.

Jay began yelling at the girls. "What are you, idiots? Be careful. Don't hit the hose nozzle on the car; you'll scratch the paint. How stupid can you be?"

Catherine and Jay would start talking again and then Jay would notice something else the girls did that irritated him and he would scream. "You idiots. You need to rinse it better than that. I don't want to have to do it over again." Then he ended each yelling session by stating to Catherine, "They're so stupid. They're just like their Mother."

Jay told Catherine stories of how his ex-wife didn't know how to change the oil, check the air in the tires and when he tried to teach her, she wasn't interested.

Catherine explained, "I don't know how to change the oil and I have no desire to learn."

"That's different. You aren't married to someone who has a hobby of being a car mechanic. I love spending time working on my cars. Here I am with all this knowledge about cars and my ex-wife just refused to learn."

"I don't blame her. I wouldn't have wanted to learn either."

Jay told Catherine about once when he was married, on his wedding anniversary, he called his wife from work and told her he would take her out for dinner that night. He said, "I pulled in front of the house and honked. She came running out wearing a skirt and sweater. Can you imagine that? I told her to go right back in the house and put on a dress. She knew I would be wearing my suit from work and she knew we were going to a nice restaurant. Really, no respect for me at all. A skirt and sweater!"

Jay continued to yell at his daughters, calling them, "idiots," and "stupid," or saying, "How dumb can you be?" Again he would follow it by saying to Catherine, "Just like their Mother."

Jay told Catherine the Bible says women were put on this earth to obey their man. Catherine was thankful they had different Bibles. She wondered if his Bible mentioned skirts and sweaters.

After one glass of tea, Catherine knew why he was divorced. When Jay offered her a second glass of tea, she declined and told him she had to pick up Molly from her friend's house and then they were going to visit another friend for the day. Catherine saw no point in spending another second with him so her white lie came easy.

Jay sent Catherine a card that week saying how happy he was to meet her. He added he hoped they could continue to become closer.

The next Sunday Catherine sat down in mass at her usual spot, which was the third row from the front. That was the perfect spot to watch Molly as she sang in the choir. Right before mass started Jay came in and sat next to Catherine. This made her very uncomfortable and she resented he was invading her space.

He gave her a quick and inappropriate kiss on the cheek and put his arm around the pew behind her. Catherine felt like he was marking his territory. She was uncomfortable all through mass.

After mass, Catherine told Jay she and Molly couldn't talk because they were running late for some previous plans. He asked if he could see her later but she told him they were going to be gone for the day. Molly came up while they were talking and knew immediately what her mother was doing. "Let's go Mom, I don't want to be late." Bless her heart.

Jay called Catherine later that evening and left her a message. "Come one, come all. I'm having you over for a cookout on Saturday night. I've got a great menu planned. No need to bring anything but yourself."

Catherine called him back and declined.

"Okay. How about I take you out after mass next Sunday?"

Realizing he wasn't going to give up, she responded, "Look Jay, I need to tell you something. An old boyfriend has come back into my life. I want to give it one more chance. We have a lot of history."

"If it didn't work the first time, it isn't going to work the second time," Jay said.

The next Sunday Catherine sat in her usual pew. Jay came in and sat down beside her again. "Where's your old boyfriend? Doesn't he attend church?"

Catherine did not respond. As soon as mass was over, she quickly left.

The following Sunday Catherine was determined not to sit next to Jay. When they arrived at church, Molly sat down with the choir and Catherine walked around the halls of the church until she knew mass started. Then she went to the back of the church and sat down, noticing that Jay was sitting in her usual place. She could see a small bald spot on the back of his head.

He didn't spot her until communion time. After mass he said, "I saw Molly was here but didn't know where you were. I was getting worried."

Catherine quickly walked away.

Jay called her during the week and left her a voice mail message saying he would like to get together with her just as friends. He said he realized she was dating someone else and respected that but he saw no reason why they couldn't keep up their friendship.

On the following Sunday Catherine did the same trick as before, waiting until mass started and then sitting down, this time in a different spot in the back.

Shortly after mass started, Jay spotted her. He immediately got up and moved, plopping himself right down beside her.

Molly saw him get up to move next to her mother and knew her mother was upset. From the choir section, Molly was shaking her head back and forth in disbelief.

Catherine was livid that he was once again violating her space with this bold move. She quickly got up and moved to another pew in the church and luckily Jay did not follow.

After communion, Jay walked out the door. Catherine figured her cold shoulder sent a clear message. Since Catherine and Molly felt no need to rush off after mass, Molly went to the recreation room to get a donut and Catherine stayed behind to visit with some friends. It was nice not to feel the need to rush off. However, her freedom was short lived because the next thing Catherine knew, Jay appeared. He came over and introduced himself to her friends, acting as if he and Catherine were best of friends for a long time. Catherine's friends were ready to leave so they said goodbye and Catherine was now left alone with Jay.

"I need to get Molly. We've got to leave," she said to Jay as she walked away.

"Wait a minute. You told me your parents live in Oklahoma. I thought it would be nice for them to have a picture of you." He pulled a camera out of his pocket, flipped up the flash and aimed.

"No," Catherine objected, "They have enough pictures of me."

"Parents can't ever have enough."

At this point he put the camera up to his eye to shoot. There was no way Catherine wanted her picture taken. She wondered why he really wanted the picture. The disgusting thought crossed her mind that he probably wanted it for some sort of autoerotism on his lonely nights. She didn't want him looking at a picture of her so she held her hand over her face and at the same time saw the flash go off. Catherine started walking away as fast as she could. Jay ran to get in front of her, clicking the camera as he ran. Catherine ran into the ladies room to escape Jay and his camera. Luckily, when she came out, Jay was gone.

The next two Sundays Catherine skipped mass, dropping Molly off in the front of the church so she could sing with the choir. After mass Catherine would be waiting out front to pick up Molly. It was ridiculous but she didn't know of another way to handle it and she couldn't stand the thought of dealing with Jay or even looking at him. Catherine didn't know how long she planned on missing mass. She didn't have a plan. She just knew until she figured out what to do, this was the way she was going to handle the situation.

Jay left Catherine a message after mass, stating concern for her well-being. He wanted to know if she was all right and insisted she call to ease his mind so he wouldn't have to worry. Catherine did not return his call.

The following Sunday Jay cornered Molly. "Is your Mom okay?"

"She's fine."

"What's going on? Why isn't she here?"

"Don't worry about it. She's fine."

When Catherine found out Jay had approached her daughter, she knew she had to do something. First of all it was a shame she was letting this man disrupt her life, and the fact he was now approaching her daughter, well that was the last straw.

Catherine called Jay and luckily got his answering machine. She left a message telling him he made her very uncomfortable and she had a boyfriend and her boyfriend objected to Jay trying to sit with her and she herself objected to him constantly harassing her. Catherine told him he had no right to approach her daughter and he needed to leave Molly alone. She also told him she did not consider him a friend and she barely knew him and would appreciate it if he would respect her enough to leave her and her daughter alone. Of course, he did not.

Later that afternoon, Catherine was sitting on her front porch, looking at a magazine when Jay pulled up in her driveway. As soon as Catherine saw him, she got up, went inside and locked the front door.

He stood at the front door and yelled, "We need to talk. Open the door."

Catherine yelled through the door, "I'm calling the police." To her surprise, Jay immediately left.

The next week Catherine went to mass and sat in her usual place. To her relief, Jay wasn't there, which thrilled her. When she got home, there was a small bouquet of carnations with a note stating, "I just want to be your friend. I miss not sitting with you in mass." Catherine did not respond.

Believe it or not, this has a happy ending as far as the church seating goes. Catherine never heard from Jay again and to this day he has never appeared at Sunday mass. She doesn't know what happened to him but she just loves happy endings. It could be God didn't want Jay sitting beside her either. After all, He has the final say regarding His seating chart.

SEATING CHART ADDENDUM

Catherine's daughter, Molly, is now four years older than she was when the story *The Seating Chart* took place. A young girl's appearance can change tremendously over the course of four years and Molly, who was a cute young girl, was now a striking beauty.

Molly was working at a restaurant as a waitress. One of the new waitresses came over and told Molly, "My Dad thinks you're cute." Molly told her thank you for the compliment and continued to wait on her tables. A minute later, the waitress approached Molly again and said, "My Dad wants to talk with you." Molly reminded her she was busy working her own section of tables so couldn't talk with her Dad. Shortly after that, the new waitress approached Molly a third time and exclaimed, "My Dad is getting mad at you. Can't you at least wave at him? He'll be mad at me if you don't at least wave." ·

Molly thought this was bizarre. Molly had a boyfriend who was her own age and had no interest in this older man. However, she agreed to wave.

"There he is," the waitress pointed her father out.

After spotting him, Molly did not wave. "Tell your father he went out with my mother, Catherine." Molly figured that would embarrass Jay into not sending his daughter over to pester her anymore.

However, she returned and said to Molly, "My Dad said he didn't recognize you at first because you've changed so much. He said to tell you he never really liked your Mom that much and he thinks you're cuter. He said to tell you he doesn't have a problem dating girls your age since his last girlfriend was twenty-one."

"I have a boyfriend and I'm not interested. Don't approach me anymore about this ridiculous matter."

Catherine and Molly had a good laugh that night, thinking about what a fool Jay made of himself. However, they did admit they were shocked Jay had not backed down after finding out Molly was the daughter of Catherine. They both felt very sorry for his daughter. It's sad when a junk male is someone's father.

THE BAR SCENE

Miriam was leaving the grocery store early one morning when she heard a man yell, "You have beautiful legs." She ignored the man the first time although she was flattered. More than one man had told her that her legs were gorgeous so without looking, she knew his comment was directed towards her. Besides, it was very early in the morning. How many beautiful legs could be in the grocery store parking lot?

Again he yelled, "You have beautiful legs." This time she looked in his direction and saw him coming towards her. He looked to be in his late fifty's, was wearing black slacks and a black turtleneck sweater with a black leather jacket. He had a neatly trimmed beard with streaks of gray giving him a very distinguished appearance. She thought he looked very notable with a warm inviting smile that seemed familiar.

He immediately apologized for his crude approach to obtain her attention but defended his comment by explaining she did have beautiful legs and he just couldn't think of anything else to quickly say before she got away. For some reason, his explanation put her at ease.

"I normally don't hit on lovely ladies so early in the morning."

"Really? What time of day do you hit on lovely ladies?"

Laughing he responded, "Okay. Duly noted. You'll have to excuse me. I'm not thinking straight. I should be forgiven for anything stupid I say. Especially before having my first cup of coffee."

"No coffee yet?" Miriam sympathized. "You must have really needed something at the store to go out without your morning cup. You wouldn't have caught me noticing anything without at least two cups of coffee in me. What grocery store emergency brought you out so early in the morning?"

"I hate to tell you. Especially since I can tell you work out. You won't think highly of me."

"Try me," Miriam responded.

"Donuts. I wanted donuts," he laughed as he opened his little white bag and revealed the sugary delights.

Miriam started laughing. "I knew I liked you. I love donuts. What kind are they?"

"One sprinkled, one maple and one chocolate." He leaned forward, looked at her with puppy dog eyes and whispered in her ear, "Don't judge me."

Miriam broke out laughing. "How can I truly judge if I don't even know your name?"

"Nathan. My name is Nathan. What about you?"

"Miriam."

"Miriam" he repeated. "What a wonderful name. Nice to meet you Miriam."

"Nice to meet you Nathan."

"I don't suppose I could talk you into joining me for an early morning donut. We could sit right over there on that public bench so you would feel safe. I'll even let you have first choice on the donuts. How about it?"

Miriam hesitated for a moment before answering. She really did want to stay but had a full day of errands that needed to get done. Plus, she didn't want to seem too eager.

"Not today Nathan. I'm running on a tight schedule as it is." Miriam knew there was no way Nathan was going to let her go without someway to contact her. They were both having too much fun flirting.

"Alright then. How about your phone number? I may buy more donuts in the future and I really wouldn't feel right not sharing. Now every time I even look at a donut, I'll be thinking of you."

"Couldn't you think of me when you look at a supermodel? I'm not so sure I want donuts to remind you of me."

"Alright but I have to warn you, I see more donuts than I do supermodels."

Miriam was delighted. He was handsome and had a sense of humor. She had hit the jackpot.

"Okay. Maybe I'll take you up on your offer in the future. Of course, I have to warn you, I might want two donuts."

"Duly noted, two it is."

"Well, I've got to run Nathan. It was really nice meeting you."

"It was nice meeting you too."

Miriam glanced in the direction of her car, a signal she was definitely leaving.

"Not so fast. Do you have a business card with you?" Nathan inquired.

"No. Do you?"

"Wait a minute Miriam. I have a pen and paper. You can write your number down."

"Why don't you give me your business card and I'll call you. I'd feel more comfortable doing it that way."

"Are you sure? I have a pen right here."

"I'm sure," Miriam firmly answered.

Nathan pulled a business card from his wallet and quickly gave it to Miriam, who just as quickly secured it in the zippered part of her purse. She had every intention of following up with a phone call to this handsome, witty man who was obviously as attracted to her as she was to him.

"Thanks. I've got to go. It was really nice meeting you Nathan. Enjoy your donuts," she said smiling as she backed away.

Later that morning, Miriam met Katie for brunch. Thrilled with the news of the new man in her life, Miriam rapidly produced Nathan's business card from her purse. According to the card, he was CEO of a large well-known company. The funny thing was that as Miriam read his name to Katie, Katie thought she had heard his name before. Once Katie said that, Miriam agreed the name really did sound familiar. It didn't matter anyway. Miriam was on a high and couldn't wait to have more contact with Nathan. She believed everything happens for a reason and being out of milk that morning could be the best thing that ever happened to her. Plus, she was very proud of how she played it with him. She was flirtatious but not desperate. It was the perfect beginning.

That evening, Miriam couldn't wait any longer. She didn't want to seem too enthusiastic but really wanted to talk with Nathan. She decided to call Katie and get her opinion on if it was too soon to place a phone call. She hated playing the waiting game but hated not speaking with him even more. As she reached for the phone, it rang. It was Katie with some, as she put it, "Disturbing news." She remembered where she had heard Nathan's name. It was on the news.

"The news? What was he on the news for? Charity work?"

Even as Miriam said charity work, she knew it was something else not as flattering. After all, charity work would not be disturbing. There was a part of her who wanted her friend Katie to shut up. There was a part of her who didn't want anything to bring her off of her high.

Reluctantly, Katie enlightened Miriam.

"It happened many years ago. I was racking my brain all day trying to remember why his name sounded familiar and it finally came to me. Don't you remember he was the guy who embezzled money from his company? He stole hundreds of thousands of dollars. Don't you remember?"

"No. I don't remember any of this," Miriam firmly stated.

"I can even remember you telling me how handsome you thought he was, even back then. You said it was a waste of a hunk and you even joked about conjugal visits."

"No. That can't be." Miriam defended her lack of memory.

"Think back Miriam. Do you remember us talking about him years ago? You do, don't you? It was the very same company that was on his business card."

"But what about the business card? He had his phone number on it. He wanted me to call. He wouldn't have given me a company card with a number where he didn't work."

"I don't know. Maybe he had new cards printed using his old title, the company name with his home phone number. People can get cards printed to say anything they want."

Miriam already knew this fact but just didn't want to admit it to Katie.

"I have to go. I need to check some stuff. I'll call you later Katie."

Miriam quickly hung up the phone not giving Katie time to respond. She then ran to her computer and did a search for information.

Sure enough, there was the story about the missing funds along with a big picture of Nathan. This was the same Nathan she had been so enchanted with all day. Her memory returned. She remembered the court case and even the conversation about him years ago. Miriam felt nauseated. Next she looked up the company where Nathan supposedly worked. It was foolish to think he might have gotten his job back but she just had to look. However, there was no information to comfort her on the company web site. Not only was he not the CEO but he was not listed anywhere. And to top it off, the company had their business phone number listed and it was different than the phone number on Nathan's card.

Miriam no longer felt nauseated. Now she was mad. Mad at being lied to. Mad at being disappointed. Mad at feeling as if she were a moron. Mad her fantasies of herself and Nathan were going to be just that, fantasies. "Stupid man! You aren't even smart enough to have an alias. Any decent criminal would have had several assumed names to go by but you aren't that brilliant," Miriam said out loud to Nathan's photograph. "I guess that's why you got caught."

She thought about calling his number and telling him off but decided against it. Instead, she called Katie to share the confirmation that her Nathan was the same Nathan in the photo on the Internet. As Miriam updated Katie, she tore Nathan's card into little bits.

Katie joked with her that the next time someone yells, "What beautiful legs you have!" she should think of the story "Little Red Riding Hood" and reply, "The better to run from you with, my dear."

Looking back, Miriam was thankful she never made it to her first date with Nathan. Although, she felt it was sad not being on that high that a man can bring to your life. She was determined to find someone to share her life with and this was nothing more than a bump in the road. The right man was out there and she would just have to find him. She made a great income and was very independent. No man was needed. A man was more of a bonus to her life, not a necessity.

The next week, Miriam decided she wanted to get out of her house and check out a new nightclub. It would be the perfect place to meet someone new. Unfortunately, all her friends had plans. It was Saturday night and she now found herself in her drawstring sweat pants standing in front of her freezer staring at a tub of chocolate peanut butter ice cream.

"No! Move away from the ice cream," she screamed at herself. "I don't need my friends to have a nice time. I can go out without them."

Quickly she slammed the freezer door and sprinted up to her second floor to take inventory of the clothes in her closet. She was proud of her determined attitude to get out of the house.

At first she slipped on a short black dress but then decided that it would be best if she didn't look as if she were trying so hard. Better to be underdressed tonight. She settled on her tight black jeans, black suede high heels and a very plunging v-shaped neckline blouse in a rich burgundy. She studied herself in the mirror. She looked sexy but not desperate. Miriam was happy to be trading an evening of ice cream and guilt for an evening of socializing, dancing and hopefully a different kind of guilt the next morning.

The club was packed. The parking lot was full so she ended up parking her car a block away and walking. Her shoes were extremely beautiful but her feet were already hurting by the time she reached the front entrance to the club. She wished she had used the Valet parking.

Upon entering the club, she spotted a small table for two hidden away in the back of the club. All the prime tables by the dance floor were taken. She rapidly headed directly for the table to get off her aching feet. She wanted to save her feet for dancing.

Almost immediately after sitting down, a man approached her. He was not very polished in appearance, wearing a wrinkled shirt and scuffed shoes. He had short sideburns and coarse short brown hair that looked as if it needed a trim around the edges. Appearance wise, he wasn't anything she would usually be attracted to but she had been out with enough pretty boys and they hadn't worked out so she was keeping an open mind. Plus, a change in clothing style can always be accomplished with a little influence. Besides, she was happy to have the attention. It would have been awkward for her to sit there alone with none of her friends. She welcomed his company.

His name was Gordey and he spent most of the evening asking her questions about herself, which was a pleasant change from some of her past dates. At times, he seemed a bit awkward but he did seem to be a nice enough man. When Miriam decided to call it a night, Gordey walked her to her car. No goodnight kiss was attempted but that was okay by Miriam. She was tired and found Gordey much more appealing in the dark of the club. They made plans to meet for a casual lunch the next day. Miriam would be able to get a better idea of her feelings for Gordey at that time.

When Miriam got home, she called Katie and confessed she suspected Gordey was seeing someone else, married or maybe it was something along a totally different line such as being ashamed of whatever he did for a living. He might have felt Miriam was out of his league and been intimidated to reveal his true self to her. Miriam, being a journalist, was determined to go to her luncheon and figure out what it was about Gordey that bothered her.

The next day, during lunch, every time Miriam asked questions about his life, he would just say he was much more interested in her since he already knew everything about himself. Their conversation was at times strained and evasive when it came to her asking him questions. He couldn't tell her what he had been doing the last few years. He was avoiding all her questions, and she just knew something wasn't right.

Through her probing questions he finally broke down and admitted he had only been out of prison for a few months. He was a model prisoner and was released early for good behavior. He explained he had done his time and was ready for a clean-cut life. No more crime. He loved his mother and didn't want to disappoint her or cause her any more suffering on his behalf. Gordey told Miriam he wanted to be totally honest and up front with her.

Out of curiosity, Miriam wanted to know the details of his crime.

"Was it a white-collar crime?" she probed.

"I guess."

"You don't know?"

"Yea, I know. I was wrong and never want to go to jail again. It was the hardest thing I've ever gone through in my life. I didn't get to keep the money so it was all for nothing."

His confession was genuinely sincere. He was sorry he got caught and sorry he didn't reap the financial benefits.

Miriam decided she didn't need to know anymore. She excused herself quickly, slipping out the front door. She told Katie she was through with men for a while.

Of course Katie knew what that really meant. She knew Miriam was through with men until the next good opportunity arose to find a decent man.

The following week, Miriam had a business conference to attend. During a break at the meeting, she walked up to a group of her co-workers who were talking with another attendee at the conference. As she listened to him speak, she found him not only inspirational, but also to be an extremely intelligent, interesting man, who was a refreshing change from the last two jailbirds she had met.

Miriam observed his striking good looks and polished appearance, from his shiny silver hair to his fitted Italian suit. Plus, he was so buff. She could tell he was certainly a man who took pride in his appearance. His body was sculpted. When she looked at him, she was glad she had kept herself in great shape over the years. There was no way Miriam was going to let him out of her sight until she had a chance to introduce herself. Miriam made a point to say hello to him before the conference was finished.

His name was Jim and after a quick introduction, he said he would like to get to know Miriam better and asked if she would join him for a cup of coffee. Miriam was delighted. They ended up going to a little café across the street from the function.

Jim had been divorced for eight years, had a son named Matt but did not see him very often because Matt lived in California. Jim was currently working as a financial consultant. He enjoyed his job, although at times it was very challenging. The conversation flowed as they discussed traveling, politics, work out routines, favorite books and numerous other subjects. He was obviously very well read. Jim was the breath of fresh air Miriam had been longing for in her life. Miriam said they talked for over two hours and time flew by fast. Before they departed, she and Jim exchanged business cards and made plans to go out to dinner the following Saturday night.

On Saturday night, Jim picked up Miriam at her house and they went to Ruth's Chris Steak House. He ordered the veal and she the petite filet with shrimp, which was her favorite. She found she was too excited to eat more than a few bites. He ordered a fine vintage wine to accompany their meal. When it was time for desert, Jim reviewed the menu and declared there was only one obvious choice, the chocolate sin cake. They found they were so entranced with each other they didn't even notice the restaurant had closed. It was the perfect evening.

After dinner, Jim walked Miriam to her front door, gave her a proper kiss goodnight and departed. She was thrilled to finally meet such a gentleman. She lay in bed that night and laughed about the other two men previous to Jim. Her luck with men was finally changing.

The next morning Jim called to let her know how much he enjoyed their evening. Since the feeling was mutual, Miriam found herself inviting him over for lunch. He agreed to come so she quickly hung up the phone, jumped in the car and drove to the nearby gourmet deli that she knew was open early. After picking up some food, she stopped at the store to buy flowers and rushed back home. She then jumped in the shower and began working on her appearance.

Miriam was definitely on a high and could not wait to see Jim. Daydreams began to creep into her mind. She visualized the two of them going to black tie events, slow dancing as they gazed into each other's eyes. Next they were reading the morning paper over a cup of coffee and a croissant, discussing current events. On weekends they would be sailing on the Chesapeake Bay, anchoring just in time to watch the brilliant orange sunset slowly sink into the horizon. Not that Miriam owned a sailboat but after all, it was her vision and it was going to be romantic and perfect.

By the time Jim arrived, Miriam was looking great, had food and drinks set up on her screened-in porch with a nice mixed bouquet of fragrant flowers on the table. She was on top of the world. Life couldn't get much better. Miriam knew how fortunate she was with her job, beautiful home, good looks and it didn't hurt that she came from a family of money. To top off her good fortune, she was now getting ready to entertain a man she was very much interested in getting to know better. Life was good.

The doorbell rang and as she turned the door handle, she felt as if she were a young girl getting ready to go to the prom. Although her heart was pounding at the sight of him, Miriam kept her cool composure.

A good way to be relaxed was to feel confident so she decided to impress Jim with a tour of the downstairs of her large home. From her ultra modern kitchen with state of the art appliances, which were more for show since she rarely cooked, to her light, airy simplistic dining room. She could tell he was impressed. The complete downstairs had bleached oak floors. She had recently hired a decorator to do the first floor in a hue of warm neutral tones that flowed from room to room, adding a feeling of spaciousness. Her living room had a long white linen sectional sofa with a splash of pale lime green from the throw pillows. There were two beige armchairs facing the sofa and a modern white shag rug resting beneath an oversized brass and glass coffee table. It was a simplistic style that suited her. Her Minimalist art and sculpture collection was in the entryway, living room and in the large hallway downstairs. She was eager to share the details of each piece and was hoping he would be impressed.

After the downstairs tour was over, Miriam escorted Jim to the screened-in porch where their wine and food awaited. As soon as Jim saw the beautiful table setting he couldn't hold back his emotions any longer.

"I'm giving you notice. I'll be kissing you now. I can't wait. No woman should be so perfect."

He pulled Miriam close and kissed her passionately on the lips. She flung her arms around him and kissed back with a force."

"Miriam, I haven't felt this way about anyone for so long. I'm so happy we met."

"Me too," she whispered.

"You are accomplished, beautiful, everything a man could want. How is it you haven't been snatched up yet?"

"I could say the same about you. You've been single a number of years."

Laughing he replied, "Well, you never know what road will be traveled in life. My journey has been fascinating. I've been to destinations I never dreamed of. Even through bad times, I've learned many lessons."

"Me too. Every bad experience has made me wiser."

"I couldn't agree with you more," he said as he kissed her again.

Miriam felt so secure in his arms; so protected.

"You and I here right now, Miriam. That's what counts. The past doesn't matter. It's our future that's important."

"You're right."

For the first time that day, Miriam noticed the birds sweetly singing outside.

"Have a seat. Let's open the wine," she said knowing wine was the last thing on her mind. She wanted to show him the upstairs of her home but decided it was best not to give in to her feelings too early. She wanted him to respect her. She had to stay in control, at least for now.

Jim opened the wine, pouring the perfect amount in each glass.

"A toast," he said, "To the most perfect woman."

"Yes. A toast. I was going to say to the most perfect man but on second thought, I agree with you. A toast to the most perfect woman," she replied flirtatiously.

Jim laughed, clinking his glass with hers to seal their toast.

Miriam thought about how her life had changed so suddenly from two ex-convicts to a remarkable man. She decided to share her story about the last two men. For a joke she teasingly said, "So how long have you been out of prison?"

"What?"

"How long have you been out of prison?"

"Out of prison?"

"You heard me. How long have you been out of prison?" she repeated with a flirty smile.

"Oh shit! How'd you find out?"

"I have my sources. Now tell me all about it."

"Miriam, you knew this and you still had me over anyway?"

"Of course. Sometimes nice girls want a bad boy." She found it very cute he was playing along.

"Is that right?" he said smiling.

"Yes, that's right."

"Well then you're in for a treat because I can be very bad."

He got up, took her by the arms and pulled her up from her chair. Wrapping his arms around her again, he thrust his tongue in her mouth.

She kissed back but realized if she wanted to take it slow, she needed to pull away. "Slow down. Not right now bad boy. Let's sit down and talk first."

"Oh Miriam, you don't know how happy you're making me."

"The feeling is mutual. Now confess your sins. I want to hear all about it," she continued her game. "I find bad boys very intriguing."

"This day is working out better than a dream."

"Okay. Now tell me all about it. I want to hear everything."

"Right now? Can't it wait?"

"Yes. Right now. I need to know your side of the story," she teased.

He sat back down and had another sip of wine. "First tell me. Was it that damn Sadie?"

"Sadie?"

"Was Sadie the one who told you? Did she follow me here last night?"

"Was Sadie the jealous prison warden who was so obsessed with you that she followed you from prison to my house?"

"Prison warden? What are you talking about?"

"Everything. I know it all. She told me every single detail so we're going to have to have a little talk before we can go any further."

"She was never a prison warden. Why would she tell you that? I've had it with her."

"What?"

"Oh God Miriam. I'm so sorry. I never meant for you to find out like this." He poured himself more wine and topped off her glass too. "Let me explain," he pleaded in a serious tone.

Miriam looked at his panicked face and wasn't sure she liked the way her little game seemed to have taken such a serious turn. She no longer felt like playing. She didn't like her game anymore. Something about him was now making her uncomfortable.

Taking her hand he said, "That damn Sadie. She followed me again didn't she? Was she over here earlier? She's a jealous bitch. I suppose she told you about the Hepatitis C and crabs too."

"What? What did you say that for? That's a turn off." she pulled her hand away from him. Her game was no longer fun.

"Oh crap! I was afraid something like this would happen. She'll do anything to wreck my happiness. She thinks I owe her. Well I owe her nothing," he said with his voice starting to rise.

"What are you yelling about?" she asked suspiciously still not wanting to believe what she was hearing.

"Oh hell. What the hell did that bitch tell you?"

"I'd rather hear it from you," she demanded anxiously.

"You need to understand. I don't know what she told you but it's all manageable. I never gave her anything. As a matter of fact, I'm sure it was the other way around. The hepatitis C and crabs, it doesn't have to change anything. Like I said, it's manageable and the crabs are gone. That was weeks ago."

Miriam felt nauseated. She picked up her glass of wine and took a large swallow.

"Listen, it doesn't have to change anything if you don't want it to. You're the one I'm interested in, not her."

Miriam was shocked, not believing what she had just heard. She wanted this nightmare to end. Surely this couldn't be happening.

"Why don't you tell me your side of the story," she said. Looking outside, she noticed a bird had pooped on the screen door to the porch. Damn birds.

He started pouring his heart out to her about his troubles. Apparently he was living with a woman named Sadie since his release from prison. Lately they had been fighting a lot so Sadie said she was kicking him out of her house. He didn't know what he was going to do since he had nowhere to go. Sure he could get an apartment by himself but as he explained, he was not the type to be without a woman. He enjoyed the companionship of a female and couldn't see the benefit of living alone. After all, he had spent enough time in jail without a woman.

"I've spent the past several years incarcerated for a crime that was all a big misunderstanding."

"What type of misunderstanding?"

"It had nothing to do with any horrible crime."

"There are crimes that aren't horrible?"

"Well, it didn't have anything to do with rape or killing anyone."

Miriam did not find comfort in those words. "White-collar crime?" she asked.

"Yes."

She didn't know why but she was relieved. She wasn't sure she even knew which category all the crimes fell into but hearing white collar made her think of a crime of money, not more severe crimes. It seemed to be more of an upper-class crime. A crime of money was bad enough but it could be much worse. Of course harm had to come to someone in order for him to have been incarcerated.

Jim continued to say he didn't know for sure how he got the Hepatitis C or the crabs but he suspected it could have been Sadie. Again he emphasized it was manageable. He told Miriam there was nothing for her to worry about because he had slept with many women and as far as he knew, none of them had come down with any diseases. He explained, "There's plenty of really bad stuff out there and I can assure you, I'm upfront with nothing to hide." He continued to say since the two of them were getting along so well, and since Miriam had such a nice big home, he saw no reason why he couldn't live with her. He assured her he would live in her basement until she felt comfortable enough with him to move him upstairs. As he put it, "After all, I am a gentleman."

Miriam was shocked but also felt very vulnerable. She now had an ex-prisoner in her home. The idea he had done his time and paid his debt to society did not comfort her in the least. She decided the best thing to do was to be calm, eat lunch and get him out of there as quickly as possible without letting him know he was now seen as an intruder. She had lost her appetite but forced down a few bites, feeling she had to attempt to eat in order to mask her panic. After all, kicking him out could end up being a big mistake. She didn't know what he was capable of doing and she had no intention of finding out.

After lunch he offered to stay and help with the dishes but she declined, stating that carrying the dishes to the sink was good enough. She apologized that she had another appointment, a wedding shower for a close friend of hers, but said she would make it up to him another time. He bought her story.

Miriam walked Jim to the front door and could feel her hands trembling as she opened the door to let him depart.

"One more kiss for the road," he said as he pulled her closer.

She allowed it so as not to alert him to her change of heart.

"I'll call you later to see how your day went."

"Okay. Have a nice day yourself." She felt a sense of relief as she closed and locked the door behind him.

That night, Miriam did not answer any phone calls. Jim left two messages. One to tell her he had a wonderful time and looked forward to seeing her again and another message to say good night and sweet dreams.

Two days later, the phone rang and the Caller ID said Dr. Gessell's office. Miriam answered the phone and to her surprise, it was Jim.

"I'm at the doctor's office and figured you might have some questions about the Hepatitis C. My doctor has agreed to speak with you about it and any other concerns you might have."

Before Miriam could object, Jim handed the phone to Dr. Gessell.

"I hear you have some concerns about having sex with Jim. This call is to give you the opportunity to ask me any questions." Dr. Gessell continued, "The first thing you should do is be sure you always use a condom."

"I'm sorry but you've obviously been misled. I don't really know this man and have no intention of getting to know him better. There is no need for me to ask you any questions except maybe one."

"Anything."

"Are you really a doctor? It seems strange a doctor would let his patient manipulate him in this way. Of course, con men are known to do just that. They con people."

Dr. Gessell changed his tune very quickly as he said, "I'm so sorry. I didn't understand the situation. In no way should you ever let anyone pressure you into anything you are not ready for. I'm sorry to have inconvenienced you. Truly, I'm sorry."

There was no doubt to Miriam that Dr. Gessell was upset with Jim and very embarrassed. Miriam also wondered how Jim had persuaded the doctor to talk with her on the phone. Jim really was a good con man.

Later that day, Jim called, livid with Miriam. "Why the hell did you say that to the doctor? You made me look bad."

"I made you look bad? You put me on the spot. You were very presumptuous and how could you think any part of that phone call would be appropriate? Was that even a doctor on the phone or just a friend pretending to be a doctor?"

"It was a doctor. God, Miriam, you have to believe me. I was trying to make sure you were comfortable moving forward. I'm crazy about you. Come on, let's not miss out on something fantastic here."

"This isn't going to work."

"You can't mean that, Miriam. Is this because of something Sadie said to you?"

"It has nothing to do with Sadie. We just aren't a match."

"How can you say that? We've had nothing but great times together. Don't let one little phone call dictate our future."

"Really, Jim. I don't have time to talk. I'm running late."

"Miriam, please. Don't be that way."

"I've got to go. Bye," Miriam said as she slammed the receiver down.

For the next two months, Jim called daily but since Miriam was not taking any of his phone calls, he started dropping by her house unannounced. Even though she never opened the door, it was still unnerving.

Miriam had an alarm system installed. She'd been planning on installing one for months but never made it a top priority until now.

Unfortunately, Miriam had given Jim her business card so occasionally he would send her an e-mail. Wisely, Miriam did not respond to any of his e-mails and eventually, blocked him.

Miriam was very upset that she had contact with three men who had been locked up for criminal behavior.

Katie told her to use the word incarcerated instead of jailed. It sounded much more important and in fact, the silver lining was at least they had all been white-collar criminals. They laughed that maybe Miriam was a bit of a snob.

Miriam has now had contact with three men who spent time behind bars. It takes the expression, "the bar scene," to a whole new level.

DODGED A BULLET

Katie had a friend named Nancy who was an agent with the FBI. Many years prior, Katie fixed Nancy up on a date with a wonderful man named Fred. Fred and Nancy hit it off right away. After their first date, Fred told Katie that Nancy was going to be his wife. True to his word, Fred and Nancy were married one year to the day they met each other.

Nancy felt an obligation to consider any unattached man a future prospect for Katie. After all, finding a match for Katie would be a wonderful way to return the favor.

One day Nancy was having a bad day at work. Another agent, named Chuck, came over to comfort Nancy, even though he really didn't know her except for occasionally saying hello while passing her in the hall. Nancy felt he was very sweet for taking the time to console her.

In the course of their talking, Nancy discovered Chuck was single and asked him if he would be interested in being fixed up on a date.

Without hesitation, Chuck said, "Yes!"

That night, Nancy called Katie and encouraged her to go out with Chuck. "The FBI has some of the finest men around. Give this guy a chance."

One evening while Katie was on her way out the door, the phone rang and it was Chuck. Since Katie was running late, she didn't have a chance to talk with Chuck. However, they did talk long enough to make arrangements to go to dinner on Friday.

The weather on Friday was bitter cold and there was a chance of snow in the forecast. The snow, however, wasn't expected until much later in the evening.

Katie had hired a baby-sitter who lived right next door so she didn't have to worry about driving later that evening. The sitter was in Katie's living room, setting up a game for her and Samantha to play as soon as Katie left for her evening out.

When Chuck arrived, it didn't take long to determine he was not the man of Katie's dreams. When she opened the front door, they exchanged hellos.

"Listen Katie, it's going to snow tonight and I don't want anything to happen to my truck," he said glancing over at his shinny red vehicle. "Do you mind driving your car?"

Katie was caught off guard, hesitated and then said, "I guess I could drive."

"Good. If the weather turns bad while we're out, I don't want to worry about my truck getting damaged. You know how dangerous it can be to drive on ice with all the crazy drivers around here."

"Okay. Let me get my driver's license. It's upstairs. I'll be right back."

As Katie went up the stairs her daughter Samantha followed.

"He's history isn't he Mom?"

Laughing because her daughter knew her so well, she replied, "Yes."

Katie decided to get this date over quickly. She drove to the Subway sandwich shop that was two blocks from her house. It was the perfect decision in her mind because it was geographically close and had great sandwiches that would be made on the spot. No chitchatting at a table while impatiently waiting for their order to be cooked and served. They could get in, order, eat and she would be home in no time.

After they ordered their sandwiches, Chuck pulled his billfold out, turned to Katie and said, "I'll get it tonight. You can get the next one."

Katie wondered why she hadn't told Chuck that she thought his suggestion she drive was rude. She wondered why she was so polite to a man lacking manners. She guessed it was because she was trained from childhood to be polite. Maybe that would be something she would have to change. Being proper isn't always what it's cracked up to be.

Chuck informed Katie he had been dating a woman for a very long time but they had just broken up. He told her his former girlfriend usually insisted on paying for the meals when they went out.

"It's sounds like you had a good thing with her. Maybe you should consider going back," Katie suggested.

"Nah! I think I can do better. I'm off to a good start with you."

Katie was very pleased she was driving because that put her in control. In no time at all, they had finished their sandwiches and were ready to depart. Katie immediately drove straight home.

"You're headed home?" Chuck asked in amazement.

"Yes I'm concerned about my car too. I don't want to be out if it starts to snow and the roads get icy."

"We could head right back if the weather changes."

"No. I don't want to take any chances."

His concern for her car was obviously not as great as it was for his own truck.

After parking her car, she quickly jumped out and practically ran for the front door. Katie stopped at the door and told him goodnight. As she was thanking him for the sandwich, Samantha opened the door. Katie was thrilled because now she had an easy out on dealing with Chuck trying to kiss her. Chuck appeared annoyed at Samantha for invading their private time.

"Are you coming in Mom?" Samantha impishly asked.

"Yes, I'll be right there."

"What? The evening doesn't have to be over. I'm coming in aren't I?"

"No, I never allow men in the house when my daughter is home."

"It's not going to hurt her."

"That's my rule."

"I think you can break your rule tonight. I've barely got to spend any time with you. I'm leaving town tomorrow and won't be back for two weeks. This is our only chance to get to know each other."

"Sorry, I need to get in."

"Just like that?"

"It looks like it's going to snow. You'd better get going now if you want to beat the storm. You don't want anything to happen to your truck."

Chuck glanced upward, studying the clouds. "Listen Katie, why don't I come in for a little bit. Like I said, I'm leaving town tomorrow."

"I already told you, I don't allow men in the house."

"Oh, come on. Don't be like that."

Katie was tired of this exchange and saw no reason to further debate with him.

"I'm letting too much cold air in the house. Gotta go." Katie quickly closed and locked the door, glad to be rid of him.

The next evening Chuck called.

"I thought you were out of town," Katie said.

"I am. I'm calling from the hotel. I just can't stop thinking about you. I'm on such a high because you're really great. I'd like to make plans for us to go out again when I get back."

"I'm sorry Chuck but I can't. I just don't feel we're a match."

"What? How can you tell already? You shouldn't be so quick to judge. We didn't spend any amount of time together. There is no possible way you could tell this soon. You're the reason the date ended so soon. I wanted us to spend more time with each other."

"Look, it's more than that. My old boyfriend called and we saw each other today. We're getting back together."

Okay, Katie knew it was an easy out but a girl's gotta do, what a girl's gotta do.

"You're really bursting my bubble. How can you be like this?"

Katie signaled for Samantha to ring the front door.

"Oh, I gotta go. That's him now."

Luckily, Chuck never called back.

Katie had forgotten about Chuck until one day when she was reading the paper and saw him in the headlines. Over the next year, she read about Chuck's troubles. Apparently the FBI fired him for fraudulent work on reports at his job. While working with the FBI he stole holsters, night-vision goggles, tear-gas and other equipment. He was also found to have been stockpiling hundreds of boxes of ammunition in the basement of his home.

Katie read where the police were called to Chuck's house on a domestic abuse matter. He was also suspected of setting fire to his house. The fire ended up destroying his home because the fire department couldn't get close enough, due to the explosive collection of stolen FBI ammunition. The sheriff's deputies ended up arresting him.

Later Katie read Chuck received a six-month prison term. He didn't make the FBI's *Ten Most Wanted* list but he certainly made her *Ten Least Wanted* list.

FRENCH TOAST

On Thursday night, Miriam decided to go to a singles party. She hadn't been there more than a few minutes when a man with whom she was acquainted, asked her to dance. Even though she was at the party to mingle and meet new people, she had a weakness when it came to dancing. Besides, in all honesty, she would usually stand around talking with the same people she already knew. This evening was no exception. Once again she found herself dancing with a male friend and having the time of her life. Miriam and her male friend were excellent dancers. There wasn't any music they couldn't dance to and they looked like a couple who had been together for years.

After nine dances in a row, Miriam was burning up and excused herself to go outside and cool off. The air immediately cooled her down since it was an extremely crisp evening. As Miriam stood outside by the revolving lobby door, a man came outside and lit up a cigarette. He was very exotic, wearing a red silk shirt that most men wouldn't be able to pull off. His hair was black, slicked back with gel and pulled into a long ponytail in the back. He had high chiseled cheekbones. He looked as if he could have been a male model straight off the cover of *GQ* magazine. He noticed Miriam studying him so she immediately looked away, embarrassed for being caught.

"That's alright, look if you like. I saw you inside. You have been dancing all evening," he said with his French accent.

"I love to dance." She also loved his sexy accent.

"There are other activities besides dancing for enjoyment."

Miriam did not respond.

"You dance with passion. I'm attracted to passion."

Miriam was flattered although she didn't take the compliment seriously. She already knew this man was a player.

"You know, there is a reason I came out here to smoke."

"It's a no smoking party."

"True. But I came out here for my destiny."

"Really," she responded knowing where this was going.

"We are destined to be together this evening."

"Only this evening? How about tomorrow evening?" Miriam joked.

Smiling he responded, "We can do tomorrow night too if you want. I am a great lover. It's only natural you'll want more."

Miriam knew this kind of ego. She had known his kind of charm in the past. She would have been much more attracted to him if she were younger and more naive. In all honesty, she was still very attracted to him but knew better.

He continued, "We have chemistry. We are meant to share a bed tonight. And, as I said, tomorrow too, if you like."

He moved in closer.

"You have beautiful eyes," he said as he dropped his cigarette and crushed it gently with his shoe. "I want you."

Miriam felt it was a scene straight out of a cheap movie. Of course in the movie, they would probably be in a passionate embrace and a moment later, stripping off their clothes as they moved towards the bed. For a moment, she let her mind wander, dreaming of an outcome different than her sensible reality.

He was close enough that she could feel herself getting excited. Maybe it wouldn't be so bad to go down a dead end path for one night. She didn't even have to give him her real name. Sex for the sake of sex. It had been years since she had an evening like that and there was a bit of an appeal of the unknown.

He got an inch from her face and whispered, "Destiny. Do you feel it? I know you do. I saw it in your eyes from across the dance floor. You were looking at me in there and I knew we had a moment. It was the moment that drew me out here to you. I knew why you came outside. You wanted me in private."

Of course that wasn't why she was outside, but it didn't matter. There was something about him that excited her to a point she herself didn't understand. Maybe it was his accent. Maybe it was his confidence or maybe it was his dark penetrating eyes. It didn't matter to Miriam.

Her heart was now racing. If he didn't kiss her within the next second, she was going to kiss him. She had his number but didn't care. She found the moment exciting and decided to go with it and see where the evening took her.

"Our making love will be good for you and your dancing partner. I find it makes my marriage stronger, more passionate. It keeps us alive. Do you want to feel alive?"

"You have a wife? You're married?"

"It's not a problem. You Americans always act so shocked. You do the same thing. You just sneak around and hide. It's not healthy to hide."

Miriam was no longer amused. Married men were always a turn off. She was now angry. She was angry he was married. She was angry because he had just snapped her out of her vision of passion. She was angry because he was slamming Americans in his snooty way. Why did he have to be married? She wondered if maybe she was mad at him for his honesty. His honesty killed her mood. She was ready to lash out at him for ruining her fantasy.

"You said I saw you and we had a moment when I was inside dancing?"

"Yes, from across the dance floor, our eyes locked. It's destiny."

"So all of this is because you thought I was interested in you?"

"Yes. I saw you looking at me."

Miriam started laughing; amused at the truth she was ready to reveal. She was not the least bit interested in this married playboy. She was ready for him to be a playboy, just not a married one.

"I hate to ruin your special moment with me but you're wrong. The truth is that I ripped my contacts before coming to the party so I can't see more than a few feet in front of me. I guess it really isn't destiny."

"I know you saw me."

"Sorry. Go home to your wife. I'm not interested."

Miriam suddenly became aware of the cool night air. Without saying another word, she turned around and went back to the party.

She had a feeling he felt it getting colder too.

SOWING OATS

Meg and Mike were husband and wife. One day Mike brought home a buddy of his named Sy. Mike and Sy hadn't seen each other in years and Mike thought it would be great to catch up over one of Meg's famous spaghetti dinners.

During dinner, Sy disclosed his wife had left him a note on the mantel stating she no longer loved him and was leaving. Sy was very distraught because he thought he was going to be married for life and wasn't even aware there was any trouble in his marriage until he found the goodbye note. Sy was at a loss as to what went wrong.

As soon as Meg heard Sy's story, her mind started churning ideas around to help bring Sy out of his depression. It didn't take Meg long to think of her single friend Katie. Meg suggested to Sy he needed to move on with his life and she thought she had someone who would be great for him. She told Sy she would handle the arrangements.

The next day, Meg called Katie to update her on her new find. Meg told Katie that Sy had a nice head of wavy dark brown hair and an extremely sculpted body from his obsession of working out at the gym. He was very outspoken but seemed to be nice. She said Sy told her he really wanted to have someone in his life and was very lonely. He also said he had finally come to the realization that reconciliation was never going to happen. He was ready to start dating.

The plan was that Mike, Meg, Sy and Katie would all meet at McCormick and Schmick's in Reston, Virginia for drinks and appetizers for an easy get acquainted meeting. In other words, Katie and Sy would have an informal chance to check each other out before going on an official date.

Katie arrived at the restaurant first, and then Mike and Meg arrived. Sy arrived late. He was a few inches shorter than Katie.

Katie remembered going out with a short man years ago. He took her dancing on their first date. She recalled when the music changed to a slow dance her date remarked, "What a perfect fit we are," to which she thought to herself, "It would be perfect if I were breast feeding you." Short men did not appeal to Katie. She found she usually lost her good posture plus hated feeling bigger than a man, regardless of the direction, up or out. However, at least Sy wasn't as short as the slow dancer man.

Sy had an elongated nose that seemed to dominate most of his face. Due to his strong outgoing personality, the conversation easily flowed, with Mike and Sy telling funny stories of when they were younger and working together.

Meg and Katie shared with Sy some of their girls' night out stories. Of course there hadn't been any of those nights in years since Meg was married; she no longer had an interest.

After a drink and splitting several appetizers, Sy asked Katie if she would like to stretch her legs and walk around Reston Town Center. The Pavilion had a concert and he thought it might be fun to check it out. That was the signal he liked her. Meg and Mike left to go home and Sy and Katie left to stretch their legs.

They had a great evening as Sy talked about his family and asked questions about Katie's family. He did talk about his ex-wife a little too much so Katie asked him how long he had been divorced and was surprised when he answered, "officially since Wednesday." This was Friday so she could see why it was still on his mind.

Overall Katie had a really nice time with Sy. They had been together for a total of four hours now and Katie decided to call it a night. He asked for her phone number, which she promptly gave to him. As they headed out to find her car in the parking garage down the block, Katie was thinking to herself this was the first time a fix up date had gone really well. She was looking forward to getting together with Sy again. She was thinking how nice it would be if they ended up a couple. Here is this man who was all depressed about his divorce and thinks he'll never get over it, and here she was thinking she would never find the right man for herself and then they meet. His divorce could end up being the best thing to ever happen to both of them.

When they arrived at Katie's car, she told Sy goodnight and she was really pleased they met. She hesitated a moment to see if he was going to give her a good bye hug or some intimate gesture before she got into her car. When he didn't move closer, she leaned over to him and gave him an appropriate kiss on the cheek and said she hoped to see him again.

Sy exclaimed, "What? Are you kidding me?"

"What do you mean?"

"Don't pretend we don't have something here."

"I think we do have something here" Katie replied honestly.

"Then where do you think you're going? Stop the game playing."

"What are you talking about? I'm not playing a game."

After a huge sigh, Sy responded by saying, "Let's put our cards on the table. I have a really big house, I'm lonely and I think you're beautiful. Come back to my place and spend the night."

"Is that all you want?"

"For tonight it is."

Katie looked at Sy in astonishment, not believing how the last minute of their time together had taken such a quick turn.

"Come on Katie, you know you want to. We both do."

"I've only known you a few hours? And I'm looking for something more than a one night stand."

"A one night stand? Come on honey, we can make it several nights if that makes you feel better."

"This conversation is over," she said as she flung open the car door.

"I'm sorry, I didn't mean it," he quickly responded. "It's just you're so beautiful I couldn't help myself. I probably wouldn't have known what to do with you once I had you there anyway."

"You do the same thing with me you did with your ex-wife only because it's new, you'd stay awake a little longer."

Katie was furious, slammed the car door and no longer paid any attention to him. She was very disappointed.

About a week later Katie got a voice mail message from Sy. He stated he bought a book on Notre Dame he thought her Dad might enjoy reading. Sy remembered Katie saying her Dad was a big fan. He wanted to mail it to her so she could give it to her Dad when she went home for Christmas or he wanted her address so she could deliver the book to her Dad.

Katie waited until the next day when she knew Sy was at work. She knew he probably wanted her address so he could stop by unannounced to see her sometime so she called his home answering machine and left this message: "Hi Sy. It was nice of you to be thinking of my Dad. Here's his address." At that point she left her father's address and hung up.

Over the Christmas holiday Katie received a package in New York, addressed to her from Sy with instructions on a note. "Give this book to your Dad from YOU." Sy had underlined and capitalized the word you. Katie wasn't sure if this was his way of keeping her in the loop so she would have to respond to him or he might have felt embarrassed to send a book to a total stranger.

Katie gave the book to her Dad and told him the story behind why he was receiving this gift.

Her Dad, with his Irish humor, opened the package and saw the paperback book and jokingly announced, "What, no hardback?" Her Dad wrote Sy a thank you note to keep Katie out of the loop.

After Katie returned home she had several messages from Sy wanting to know if her father had received the book and if he enjoyed reading about the Fighting Irish. Since Katie knew her Dad had written a thank you note, she did not respond.

A few days later, Sy left Katie a voice mail saying he would like to get together with her for dinner and a movie.

Katie returned his call. "Look Sy. I think we are at different stages. I've been single for years and I'm looking for something serious. You should go out and do the singles scene. See a lot of women. This area is great for socializing. You're going to discover how much fun you can have dating around."

"I admit, I do want to date around but I want to see you too."

"I'm not interested in being one of many. I don't want to be the girl on the backburner."

"Is that what you think? I never intended to put you on the backburner. I want you on the front burner and I'll put all the other women on the backburner."

"You aren't listening to me."

"Yes I am. I'd still like to take you to dinner and you don't even have to sleep with me."

"Goodbye Sy."

Katie has since heard Sy is completely over his ex-wife and is dating many women, most of them very young. Meg told Katie *commitment* was no longer a word in Sy's vocabulary. It looks like Sy's divorce ended up being the best thing in his life. Sy is having the time of his life sowing his oats. Katie knows Sy isn't missing her. Katie who?

THE PLAYGROUND

One day, Catherine was at the Kemper Open golf tournament. It was a beautiful day for golf. As she walked to get the next good spot for watching, a local celebrity of the Washington, D.C. area named Joe, approached her. Joe did the local news on a television station in Washington. Joe had coal black dyed hair. Catherine had heard hair stylists refer to his hair as, "the black football helmet." He had an orange glow to his skin from tanning cream. Catherine could see finger streaks where Joe had not blended the cream into the side of his neck evenly.

Joe and Catherine talked for a short while and then exchanged numbers. Through the course of their conversation, Joe found out Catherine's birthday was the following Thursday.

"Could I do the honor of taking you out for your birthday?" Joe asked.

"I'd be delighted," Catherine replied.

On Thursday evening, Joe picked Catherine up at her house, greeting her with flowers and a sweet card. Since they really didn't know each other, Catherine had not expected such grand treatment and was pleased with Joe's efforts.

On the way to the restaurant, Joe instructed Catherine she was not to mention anything about current events or news to him. He said he had enough of that at his job. He also instructed there was to be no talk of any serious matters. He noted even health issues were taboo.

Catherine made a mental note not to discuss hemorrhoids or gall bladder surgery.

During dinner they had a nice time with Catherine asking Joe about his family and Joe telling some cute stories about when he was a young boy. The evening was going so well that before dinner was finished, Joe asked Catherine to go out with him on Saturday and Catherine gladly accepted.

After dinner, Joe took Catherine to the latest hot spot nightclub in Washington, D.C. There was a long line from the entrance of the club, extending clear around the corner, but that didn't matter. Joe walked right up to the rope and was let in immediately. As he put it, "You're getting to enjoy one of the many perks of going out with a celebrity."

As soon as they entered the club, Joe was quickly escorted to one of the best tables.

"A bottle of champagne to celebrate your birthday."

"A glass will do. I drank enough wine with dinner. I'm a lightweight and can still feel a buzz."

"Nonsense. It's your birthday. You can make an exception."

When the champagne arrived, Catherine didn't want to seem rude so she took small sips but didn't drink much.

"Come on. Drink up!" Joe kept bugging Catherine.

Every time she took a sip, Joe would pour more in her glass. Joe was making such a big deal about Catherine drinking that she started getting a little annoyed with him.

The other thing that bothered Catherine was Joe knew all the young girls in the club and didn't miss an opportunity to talk with any of them. Every time a young girl walked by their table and looked his way, he would quickly jump up to say hello.

Catherine took the opportunity to pour her champagne into the large potted plant next to their table. Upon Joe's return, he looked pleased at Catherine's progress with her drinking. Of course he would promptly fill her glass up again, even when Catherine objected.

After the bottle of champagne was empty, Joe surprised Catherine by ordering another bottle. Catherine knew it was no good telling him she didn't want anymore.

Joe continued to get up from the table to talk with young girls, leaving Catherine with her friend the potted plant. Catherine actually had the impression Joe thought he impressed her with all his young groupies, but in actuality, the opposite was happening.

With Joe's continued absence, Catherine started feeling sorry for her new friend, the potted plant. She was afraid the champagne would kill it so she decided to let her remaining champagne go untouched.

Catherine had never been to this club. As she looked around, she felt a little embarrassed because she was obviously the oldest woman in sight. Most of the girls looked to be around her daughter's age and she started wondering if she would run into any of her daughter's older friends. Catherine observed that everyone in the club was wearing black so it was a good thing she selected her black dress that evening instead of her cream colored dress.

When Joe finally returned from talking with another young lady, Catherine informed him she really needed to get home.

He looked at his watch and said, "It's only one in the morning. I'm usually not home this early."

She suggested he drop her off and then go back out, an idea that seemed to please him. Catherine suspected he was eager to hang out with his groupies.

On the following Saturday, as previously planned, Catherine drove to Joe's house. Joe wanted to visit the town of Oxford, Maryland and since Oxford was in the direction of his house, Joe requested Catherine drive to his place.

On the drive to Oxford, Catherine found her opinion of Joe was not improving. He started talking about his co-workers, explaining how one woman had blue contacts but she tried to trick everyone into thinking her eyes were really that shade of blue. "Not like my eyes," he stated proudly, "Mine are naturally blue."

Catherine wondered when colored contacts became a bad thing. She did not disclose her contacts were tinted.

Joe said he intimidated the other men in his office and they were jealous of him because he always dated cute young blondes. He was afraid with his contract coming up, he had to be very careful because a lot of the men would like to see him fail. He explained television was a cutthroat business where the youngest man was the one who would succeed. He admitted he dyed his hair in order to look as young as possible.

Catherine was surprised Joe admitted to dying his hair.

Joe told Catherine he was in his thirties, which would mean Catherine was much older, but Catherine did not believe him. It was obvious Joe was much older than Catherine. She let his lie go unchallenged. Contradicting him would only hurt his feelings and she guessed he would probably deny it anyway.

"I've always looked young for my age," he bragged. "I lied on my job application but let's face it, everyone in this business lies. Besides, I have to do what is best for my career. In the show biz world, it's never wise to be any older than your thirties."

"There are anchor men older than that so what's the big deal? It's not like you're trying to be a model," she challenged.

"You wouldn't understand since you're not a celebrity. I also keep my body in tip-top shape. It's all about appearance. Why my personal trainer says I have the body of a fourteen-year-old."

Catherine wondered why Joe would think it was a compliment. Did he want the body of a fourteen-year-old?

"One of the women at the news station married an older man. I suspect it was for money. She has a diamond so big she refuses to wear it to work and keeps it in a vault. That's her way of implying she is so well off she doesn't need to flaunt it," Joe said.

"I would think wearing it would be the way to flaunt it."

"No. It's her way of letting us know she is wealthy."

"Wow. I must have a lot of jewelry in the vault too. I'm not wearing a big diamond either."

The more Joe talked, the more Catherine did not like him. He had something rude to say about everyone at his office. She wondered what rude things he would be saying about her when she wasn't around.

When they arrived in Oxford, Catherine found it a charming little town inhabited by easy-going, friendly people. The tranquility of the water was a great place for an escape from a traffic-filled hectic life.

Since it was such a beautiful day, Joe took Catherine to a little store to rent bicycles so they could peddle around and explore Oxford. They stopped at a boat building shop to visit with a friend of Joe's. As soon as they walked in, the man saw Joe and yelled, "Hello Joe and Mary. Good to see you again."

"This isn't Mary. This is Catherine."

"Oh. I'm so sorry Catherine," the man apologized. "I've seen too many of his blondes."

Joe and Catherine spent the day riding around the streets of Oxford, stopping occasionally to check out little shops. It was such a peaceful, relaxing day.

After returning the bicycles, Catherine and Joe walked to a waterfront café for some wonderful fresh jumbo crab cakes. As they sat at their outdoor table by the waters edge, listening to the ripples of water gently slap the side of the deck, Catherine thought what a wonderful time she was having with Joe. The day was better than she expected and now she was having great food in an extremely romantic setting.

As they watched the sun set on the horizon with its brilliant pink, orange and red color, she felt closer to Joe than she had ever felt. Their time in Oxford had passed quickly. It had been great weather and now it was the perfect ending to their day. Together, sharing a quiet moment, watching nature at its best, she was beginning to think maybe she and Joe would work out.

Joe must have been feeling the same sense of closeness as he gently took Catherine's hand in his own. They sat there in silence, enjoying the view.

After a few minutes, Joe said, "It's time to go."

Catherine was ready to leave. She reflected on their perfect day in Oxford's quaint, friendly atmosphere. Riding bikes, laughing with Joe, checking out small shops, wonderful fresh food and one of the most beautiful sunsets, made her feel closer to Joe. It was the kind of town that made you want to return. She couldn't ask for anymore. She knew at that moment she would be seeing Joe again. She had judged him too quickly. This man was definitely worth another chance.

As they walked hand in hand back to the car, they passed a shop that had a long black nightgown on display in the window.

"Don't wear anything like that. I don't like those long things. I like short sexy nighties best. Nothing that covers you up. I like to see what I'm getting," Joe declared.

Catherine thought it was an inappropriate presumption on his part, but said nothing. She didn't want to ruin her good mood.

"And don't wear flat shoes around me. I like high heeled shoes."

"Really, how many pairs do you own?"

There was a long pause as Joe gave her a disapproving glare.

"And don't shave yourself down there. Only porn stars do that. I don't want you furry either. Just well maintained."

Catherine rapidly snapped out of her romantic mood. Did he see nothing wrong with what he was telling her? She met his comments with silence. She no longer felt he was the type of man she wanted to get to know. She knew enough. Suddenly she wished her date with him were over and she were already at home, relaxing in her sweatpants.

On the drive back to his house, Joe told Catherine he wanted to buy a new car. He loved his Lincoln but liked to change cars every three years and asked what kind of car she would suggest.

"How about a Lexus?" Catherine said.

"Lexus? Maybe so. I might like to test drive one and see. Let's stop at a dealership on the way back."

"Won't they be closed?" Catherine asked.

"Let's stop anyway and take a peek."

When they arrived at the dealership, it was closed. They walked around the lot and looked at cars anyway. It was dark and there was a chill in the night air. Catherine wanted to go home but stayed silent.

When they finally arrived back at Joe's place, Catherine knew she needed to use the rest room before her long drive back home. As she entered Joe's house, it was apparent his place was an extension of himself. White pleather sofa, fake fig tree, shinny black plastic coffee and end tables. Everything looked cheap, uninviting and fake.

"Watch the carpet," he directed.

Catherine looked at the white carpet beneath her feet.

"Please stay on the plastic," he said as he pointed to the long narrow clear plastic laid throughout his place from room to room as a walkway. "Or, better yet, just take your shoes off. The carpet is new and I don't want anyone walking on it."

"I'll keep my shoes on. Which way to the rest room?"

"Follow the path and go left at the end of the living room and it's the first door on your right down the hallway. Stay on the plastic."

"At least Dorothy had a yellow brick road."

"What?"

"Nothing," she replied as she continued down the clear plastic road, which guided her to the bathroom entrance. Luckily there was no plastic in the bathroom so she was free to roam wild.

When she finished in the bathroom, she found herself carefully maneuvering back on the plastic. "This is ridiculous," she thought. A moment later she found herself leaping off the plastic, doing a quick gyrating carpet dance on his new carpet. "Let's see Dorothy do that on the yellow brick road," she thought laughing to herself. Catherine had her fun and was ready to take her official place, back on the clear plastic road that led to the front door.

Upon entering the living room, to her amazement, Joe was standing at the bottom of his stairway posed as he leaned against the wall with one arm. He wasn't wearing anything but a small red cup thing that covered his penis. To this day, Catherine doesn't know if he was wearing a red thong bikini bathing suit or thong underwear, but there he was in all his glory. He turned his back to her and displayed the faint hint of a red string that was lost in his butt crack.

"Like what you see?" he asked as he wiggled his bottom.

"Oh my God, what are you doing?"

His white hairless chest did not match his tan neck and face. You could see where he stopped using his tanning cream, as there was a definite color change from his short neck to his chest.

"I thought I'd give you a chance to see what my personal trainer sees," he proudly stated.

"I wish you and your personal trainer all the happiness in the world," was all she could think to say.

"Don't tease me. Do you like what you see? This is new. I have one in blue too. Do you want to see it?"

"No. I'm seeing enough with the red."

He walked over to her, freely walking on the carpet with his bare feet. For the first time, Catherine noticed Joe didn't just have a short neck but he had no neck. His body looked out of proportion. Joe put his arms around her and gave her several sloppy wet kisses. Catherine's whole face was wet which reminded her of a paper towel commercial she had seen on television. She really needed a roll right now, that is to say, a roll of paper towels.

Joe said in a deep soft voice, "Let's go upstairs and play."

"No thank you, it's a long drive. I need to get home."

"Come on. We don't have to do anything. I just want to play."

Catherine looked at him in his ridiculous red thong and thought about the juvenile word "play" and wondered how many young women had gone for that line. All of a sudden she found herself smiling. She wished his co-workers at the news station could see him now.

"I can tell you like what you see. You have the biggest smile I've seen all day." Joe was obviously misinterpreting her smile.

"It's just I'm shocked to find you in so little."

"You like it don't you?" he stated with pride.

"It's not that I don't like it, it's just I'm not in the same place you are," she politely said.

"You could be. Let's go play together. I'm very good at recess."

Catherine couldn't help but chuckle a little. After all, was recess a word he really wanted to use right now?

"Look Joe, I've had a very nice day but I really don't know you. I'm just not as fast as you are."

"That's okay, all I want to do is play. We can go slow."

"I'm sorry, but you'll have to play with yourself." She didn't mean it the way it came out but when she thought about what she had just said, she started chuckling at the appropriate comment.

"Come upstairs. I want to play."

"I need to get home." Catherine headed towards the front door.

"What? We've had a great day and you're going to leave?"

"Yes we had a great day but I'm not comfortable with going upstairs."

"Did you want to stay down here?"

"No. I'd hate to get any body prints on the new carpet."

"Don't worry about that. The plastic has plenty of room. "Come on. What are you afraid of?"

Catherine was now at the front door, opening it up when Joe stepped in front of her.

"Stop. I just want to play. Come on. Don't end the perfect day by being this way. Let's just go upstairs. We can talk."

"No Joe!"

"We don't have to do anything. I just want to play!" he started raising his voice, visibly upset she was leaving.

"All right," Catherine said in a serious tone. "Let's get out of the playground for a minute and talk like adults. You haven't even asked me if I'm on birth control? Aren't you the least bit concerned?"

"Not at your age."

As soon as the words came out of her mouth, she knew she regretted them. She had just set herself up for that response.

"Are you planning on using a condom? I'd really like to know ahead of time. Also, when was your last Aids test? Do you have the results here to see? When was the last time you slept with someone? I really need to know these things."

"You're mean. You're just mean. You've taken the romance out of everything," he whined.

"What part of this do you think is romantic?"

"Look at me. How can you want to walk away? Do you know how many women want me? Do you know how popular I am?"

"Yes. A legend in your own mind!"

He was not the least bit appealing to her in his red thong, and those sopping wet kisses that covered her face. Talk about a turn-off. Catherine walked past him to her car. As she got in, she heard him yell, "You're mean. You're just plain mean. You've ruined everything. We had a great day and look what you've done!"

It was obvious what she had done, as she could clearly see from his small thong that he was no longer excited.

Catherine wanted to turn to him and say, "Anymore talk like that young man and you'll have to sit in the corner for a time out." However, she kept her mouth shut and drove away.

Catherine heard from Joe a month later. He left her a voice mail message.

"I bought a Lexus and I hate it. This is all your fault. The Lexus doesn't have the same space as my Lincoln Town Car. You've ruined everything. I hate the car and I wish I never met you."

Maybe a little red wagon to match his little red thong would have suited him better.

DUMPED

Catherine's married friends were always in cahoots to, as they put it, "Find Catherine a husband." One day her married friend Peggy approached her and excitedly exclaimed she knew of a wonderful man named Tom who would be perfect for Catherine.

Peggy said, "He is so nice and from a very good family. I think the two of you would hit it off."

Catherine agreed to go out with Tom, who called her the next day. They decided to meet in the lobby of Clyde's restaurant in Tyson's Corner for dinner. Catherine told Tom he would be able to recognize her because she would be wearing a dark purple coat. It was wintertime, very cold and even though she had a black coat, the purple one would be easier to spot. Tom said he would be wearing his red tie.

Catherine got dressed up that night and was pleased with her appearance. She was wearing a conservative but very classy red silk dress with her favorite diamond necklace. Catherine headed for Clyde's early because she did not want to take a chance of being late due to the traffic. However, on this night, the traffic was light so she ended up arriving about fifteen minutes early.

As she stood looking out the window of the restaurant she spotted a tall, distinguished man in a red tie coming up the front steps. "I hope that's him," she thought. It wasn't. He greeted a lady with a kiss and they went off to their table. A few minutes later, Catherine saw another man with a red tie coming towards the door. He was about 5'4" tall with a thick black toupee that was a good four inches in height placed on his head. He had a huge potbelly and his shirt wasn't tucked in all the way in the front, giving him a disheveled appearance. Catherine quickly prayed, "Dear God, please don't let that be him."

As soon as the man entered, he looked over at Catherine and yelled in a squirrelly nasal tone, "Catherine, is that you?"

For a brief second she thought, "Just don't respond and walk right by him. He doesn't know it's you." Then she thought, "I'm in a damn purple coat." Catherine also thought about her married friend who had attempted this match and how it would be rude not to meet Tom. However, look at what her friend was doing to her.

As Catherine walked over to Tom to say hello, she had a terrible time keeping her eyes off of his toupee.

"Peggy didn't tell me what a fox you are," he said in a high-pitched nasal tone. "Well, it looks as if my life is looking up," he stated.

Catherine knew at his height that was the only direction he could look.

They walked to their table. Catherine had worn heels that night and was towering over Tom. She wondered if he wore the thick black toupee to add height to himself. As they walked past the hat rack, she thought, "Why don't you hang that thing up."

Catherine knew they were not a match so she wanted this dinner over with as soon as possible. She decided she would say she wasn't very hungry and just get a salad since salads are quick to prepare. However, her plan didn't work. Tom ordered an appetizer, salad, soup, and an entrée for himself. It looked like the evening was going to be a long one.

As he spoke, his whiney nasal tone was very annoying. She had heard it on the phone but thought maybe he had a cold. Now that they were meeting in person, she realized it was his natural voice and even worse sounding in person.

Tom had been going on and on with the most dull boring conversation, all about himself. He went on about his sports car too. Catherine was positive it was not a convertible, due to his toupee. He talked about living with his mother and how it was the perfect arrangement. He had the whole basement to himself and it was "a finished basement of substantial size." He said his mother let him decorate it and he even had his own private entrance. Of course it did not have a kitchen, but that was okay since, as he said, "Mother fixes all my meals."

Catherine started visualizing all of her girlfriends watching this scenario. She knew they would be laughing their heads off while listening to him talk in that whiney nasal tone. For some reason, thinking of all of her friends watching made Catherine's evening more amusing. She actually started enjoying his boring one-way conversation. With every sentence that came out of his mouth, she knew, her invisible friends were with her, laughing. She also knew a psychiatrist would probably have a field day with her way of thinking.

Catherine was having trouble keeping her eyes off that toupee. She was ashamed of herself but found she had no willpower. She wondered why anyone would ever make a toupee that big and that black. It was such a phony severe look. The answer had to be they made it for people like Tom who would purchase such an item.

Tom kept going on and on about his life with his mother, but then he switched subjects.

"I bet you wonder why I'm over sixty years old and never been married?"

Catherine was not wondering but politely answered, "Why yes."

Tom continued in his whiney nasal tone, "Well, with the first girl I dated, everything was fine until she realized I didn't make enough money, so she dumped me. The second girl I dated I thought everything was fine, but then I met her children and they hated me, so she dumped me. The third girl I dated didn't like that I was living with mother, even though I explained to her that I had my own basement with a private entrance, so she dumped me."

He kept going on and on each time talking about what went wrong and always ending with, "she dumped me."

Catherine laughed to herself thinking, "Oh yea, I want you." Catherine found herself become more and more entertained. This explanation of why he was single was a hoot. Why in the world would any man sit there and talk about all the women who dumped him? As Catherine listened to his stories, she felt herself wanting to burst out laughing. It wasn't helping that she kept visualizing all of her girlfriends watching this scenario. She was thankful she was holding back her emotions. After all, Tom was very serious about all these stories.

Catherine regained her composure and listened attentively. That is, until the last story in which he said, "And everything was fine and then I went to bed with her and she said, 'I've been with a lot of men in my life and you don't know what the hell you're doing,' and she dumped me."

It was more than Catherine could take so she burst out laughing. She thought of the girls watching her with Tom while he was telling his last story and it was just too much. The more Catherine tried to stop laughing, the more she lost control. She couldn't quit and to make matters worse, she started making noises she'd never heard before. Grotesque gasping noises were coming from her as she laughed uncontrollably.

How could he tell her about his failed sexual encounter? "I've been with a lot of men in my life and you don't know what the hell you're doing," seemed to be best left unsaid to anyone.

Catherine's laughter was now out of control. People at the surrounding tables were staring at her. She wondered what Tom had been doing with this woman. Or maybe it was what he wasn't doing. Tears were rolling down her cheeks and she just couldn't stop. She was sure her mascara was dripping down her face from the tears of laughter. Her laughter was now making her choke so she grabbed a glass of water, quickly gulping as some of the water spilt down her chin. She now had the attention of everyone at the surrounding tables. Catherine was sure she looked like a nut case, but they would be laughing too if they only knew what he had just told her.

"Are you okay?" he whined.

His whining tone didn't help. Catherine could not regain control of her emotions so she ended up excusing herself to go to the rest room. She tried to calm herself down but it wasn't working. She stood there in the ladies room, looking at herself in the mirror. Her face was red with her black mascara and eyeliner smudged under her eyes and she found her appearance made her laugh even more. In her mind, her actions were those of a terribly insensitive person but she still couldn't cease her laughter. She had to do something to help regain her composure so she started thinking sad thoughts. She thought of her puppy that died when she was a little girl and then she thought of the time a bird's nest fell from the tree and the sad reaction of the young children in the neighborhood. She was ashamed of the way she had to recover her mental faculties. Catherine fixed her face, freshened up and headed back to the table.

Upon her return, Tom was talking to the waitress. She heard him say, "I'd like two of those cakes to go and the check please."

"Two cakes to go?" Catherine repeated.

"Yes. Mother loves dessert."

"Oh, that's sweet."

"Listen Catherine, you're a beautiful lady. Just about the sexiest I've ever seen. But your table manners are lacking. I just don't think we are meant to be."

Catherine couldn't believe what she had just heard. Was this nasal toned, basement living, mama's boy rejecting her? His cycle of talking about being dumped was over. Maybe this date was a good thing for him. After all, the tables had finally turned for Tom. But as for Catherine, she guessed she'd have to tell the girls, "I thought everything was going fine, and then I laughed and made grotesque gasping noises, drooled water down my chin, and he dumped me."

OFF THE BEATEN PATH

Vince Wells probably did not expect his morning to turn out any different than any other morning. He probably thought it was going to be another peaceful dawn while jogging along the wooded path. This was his time of solitude, his time to think. But that was before Miriam and Katie spotted him heading in their direction along the jogging path. Vince's peaceful morning was about to come to an abrupt stop. Of course, as you'll see, he brought it all upon himself, but that's getting ahead of the story.

Miriam had met Vince one afternoon while she was sipping coffee and reading the newspaper at an outside café table in Bethesda, Maryland. Vince was on his bicycle and stopped to get something to drink. All the tables were taken, so he boldly asked Miriam, who was sitting by herself, if he could join her. Of course she agreed and was very pleased to have his company. After all, Vince was an extremely attractive man. She quickly checked out his hand to see if there was a wedding ring on it and luckily, there was not. They visited for over an hour and had the most enjoyable time. Before Vince left, he asked Miriam for her phone number, which she gladly gave to him.

The following week, Vince called and he and Miriam made plans to go out to dinner on Saturday evening. He was going to take her to somewhere "very special." When she inquired where that would be, he laughed and said she would have to wait.

Miriam put on a crisp silk organza black dress with a sexy low back that left no doubt she had spent many hours at the gym. To complete her alluring appeal, she slipped on her four inch Italian silk heels with a small-jeweled detail on the top. Looking in the mirror, she knew he would be proud to have her on his arm, no matter which restaurant he chose. Her ruby and diamond gold necklace and flower ruby earrings added the finishing touch.

Vince came by Miriam's house at eight sharp, but instead taking her out to dinner, he brought Chinese food. He explained he had planned a lovely dinner at The Ritz-Carlton but his plans changed when he found out he might have to take a few calls from his office. He felt it would be better to go out another evening when he truly could enjoy a relaxing dinner.

Miriam was disappointed with the change of plans, plus she had been looking forward to getting out the house for dinner, especially since she looked fantastic and was in the mood to go out on the town, but at least he hadn't cancelled their date. She comforted herself by thinking that what was important was spending time getting to know Vince, and she didn't need to be in a restaurant to accomplish this goal.

Vince wore a pager that went off several times during dinner. Each time, he would look at the pager, and excuse himself to go to his car. As he explained, his cell phone was in the car, so he would return the pages from there to have quiet isolation with proprietary and confidential business information being discussed. Miriam offered her phone to Vince and even said if he would bring his cell phone into the house, she would give him privacy during his business calls. However, Vince refused and continued his trips to his car. Vince seemed to be acting very nervous about these phone calls, but when she asked him about it, he explained he was working on a really big business proposal and if it went through, he would make a ton of money on his commission. Miriam could see why the phone calls meant so much to Vince and she understood the need for privacy when working on large business deals.

After the fourth interruption, Miriam was getting annoyed at Vince constantly getting up and going outside to return the pages, but she said nothing. She wondered if it might have been better if he had cancelled their date until a time when they could have an evening without numerous interruptions.

After returning from the fourth phone call, he told Miriam his cell phone had gone dead in the middle of an important business conversation and he didn't have a chance to finish. Again Miriam offered the use of her phone and this time, he accepted.

As Vince was on his phone call in the living room, Miriam was in the kitchen cleaning up the left over Chinese and loading plates in the dishwasher. When she finished putting her kitchen back in order, she fixed them both some hot tea to accompany their fortune cookie. She was hoping her fortune cookie would say, "Business calls are finished. Romantic evening to begin."

She stopped at the doorway to grab a beautiful tray from her buffet, with which to carry the drinks into the living room, where he was now settled. She could hear Vince was still on the phone. As she stood by the doorway, arranging the napkins, cups and saucers on the tray, she heard him say, "Look honey, don't bother me again. If you'll just leave me alone, I'll be home soon. How, can you expect me to get anything done if you keep calling me? Now please, let me get my work done, okay? No more calls."

Miriam was shocked. His business call had finished but she now realized it was only monkey business. She also knew his fortune cookie would read, "Egg roll is the only roll you will have tonight." She hesitated a moment before making her presence known at the doorway.

When Vince saw her, he quickly said, "That damn secretary of mine. She can't do anything without me."

"Your secretary is working on a Saturday night?"

"I don't usually make her but as I said, we're working on this really big project right now and it's very important."

"Really, I thought maybe you had a girlfriend or a wife."

He nervously laughed, "Don't think so. No girlfriend here."

Miriam didn't challenge him. She placed the tray on the coffee table in front of him.

"That looks great, but I think I'll wait a while. I'm still pretty full from Chinese," Vince said as he stretched his arms and leaned into the sofa back.

"What do you want to do now?" Miriam inquired.

"How about a tour of your house. I'd love to see your place."

"Sure. Oh, listen, I need to call my sister first. She wanted to stop over tonight and I forget to tell her I had company. Do you mind if I call her real quick? I'd hate for us to get interrupted."

"Go right ahead. I think we've had enough interruptions for one night."

"I'll be right back," Miriam assured him as she grabbed the cordless phone he had just used and walked out of the room and onto the back porch.

"Don't be too long. I'm ready to give you my undivided attention," Vince yelled.

Her heart was beating rapidly as she hit the redial button.

"Hello, Wells residence," answered a woman on the other end.

"Is this Mrs. Wells?"

"Yes it is."

"The wife of Vince Wells?"

"Yes."

"I need to be sure that I have the correct person. Are you the wife, not the mother of Vince who's around late fifties to early sixties?"

"Yes, that's my husband, Vince. Who is this?"

"I'm calling from his office. Did you just get off the phone with him?"

"Yes, I just spoke with him. Are you trying to find him? He should be there honey. Do you want me to call him and tell him to find you?" Mrs. Wells generously offered.

"No. Not necessary. As a matter of fact, this can wait. I've probably just missed him in the hall."

"You must have because he is definitely working tonight. Do you have his pager number? That's the only way I can reach him. He's never in his office and he always has his pager."

"Thank you, but I have his number. It's really not important. Sorry to bother you," Miriam apologized.

"No problem honey."

"Thank you," Miriam said as she hung up.

Mrs. Wells sounded like such a sweet lady. Miriam's heart went out to her, knowing Mrs. Wells was in the dark as to her husband's location. Enough was enough and Miriam was now ready to kick Vince Wells out of her house.

Upon entering her living room, Vince was nowhere to be found.

"Vince, where are you?"

"Up here." His voice was coming from her upstairs.

"What are you doing up there?"

"I hope you don't mind I started the tour without you."

Miriam was not pleased Vince was upstairs. There was plenty to look at on her downstairs level and she felt it was a bit intrusive for him to go upstairs. She headed up the stairway, eager to get rid of him as quickly as possible. When she reached the top of the stairs, she yelled, "Where are you?"

"In here," his voice called from her bedroom.

Miriam was livid. As she entered her bedroom, she was flabbergasted to find Vince, in all his glory, standing there stark naked, with a select body part up saluting her and ready for action.

"I think I'm ready for desert after all," he said with a goofy grin on his face.

"I just got off the phone with your wife."

"What?"

"Your wife. You know, the woman you're married to."

"What are you talking about?"

"You were just talking with your wife on the phone."

"No I wasn't. I told you I was talking to my secretary."

"Don't think so. I hit the redial button to see who you were talking to and guess what? I got hold of your wife."

It became quickly obvious from his body language that he was not pleased.

"You were spying on me?"

"I'm not the bad guy here!"

"What did she say? You didn't tell her I was over here did you? What did you tell her?"

"Get out."

"What did you say to her?"

"Get out!" Miriam screamed at the top of her lungs.

"Wait a minute. Let me explain. My wife and I haven't had sex in years."

"Oh that's a new one," she responded sarcastically.

"My wife laughs at me when she sees me nude. I just have to know that someone won't laugh. Will you help me?"

After that desperate attempt on his part, Miriam quickly picked up Vince's shoes along with his clothes and left the bedroom. She ran down the stairway, flung open the front door and tossed them on her lawn.

Vince ran stark naked down the stairs after Miriam. When he saw her throw his clothes out the door he said, "Now that wasn't necessary."

"Get out!"

"Well I can't very well go like this," he said as he looked down at his body. "Come on. It's a shame to have come this far and not do anything."

"Oh my God. What are you, an idiot?" Miriam screamed. "Get out!"

Vince quickly grabbed a throw pillow from her sofa and put it in front of him as he walked to the front door.

Miriam was still standing at the front door holding it open for Vince's easy exit.

As Vince passed Miriam at the front door he turned to her and said, "Come on? Let's not end it this way."

"Get out!" Miriam shouted as she shoved Vince out the door.

"Miriam, honey. Look at me. I'm standing here on your porch with nothing but a pillow."

"You're right. You're not taking my pillow," she yelled as she quickly whipped it from him, slamming and locking the front door. Flinging the pillow on the floor she stated, "That's getting burned."

Miriam watched from the window as Vince quickly picked up his slacks and put them over his bare flesh, glancing around to see if any of the neighbors were watching. Then he scooped up the rest of his clothes and threw them in his car. That was the last she saw of Vince Wells for over six months.

Now we are back to the part where Miriam and Katie were on the jogging path, taking a brisk walk in the crisp morning air. All of a sudden, Miriam spotted Vince coming in their direction.

"Remember the married man who said his wife laughed at him when he was nude and he wanted to know if I could help?" Miriam asked.

"Yea."

"Well that's him, wearing the little white shorts and no shirt, jogging this way."

"You're kidding me?"

"Nope. That's him."

"Do you think I should tell him I'd like to have a good laugh and ask if he'll let me see him nude?"

Before Miriam could answer, Vince spotted her. Now he could have jogged by and ignored her, or he could have made a rapid U-turn and gone right back in the same direction he came from, but no, he wasn't that cool. Instead, he exited the jogging path and headed straight into the forest, which of course made Miriam and Katie break out laughing. They kept up their fast pace of walking the path until they reached the part of the forest where he had headed off the path. As they looked in that direction, they saw his head peak around a large tree trunk in the distance. As soon as he spotted them looking, he quickly tucked his head back behind the large tree.

"Oh my gosh. He's hiding behind that tree," Katie laughed.

"What a loser," Miriam declared as she kept walking.

"No Miriam. This is too good to pass up. Get back here," Katie demanded as she stopped in her tracks and faced the tree. "Don't let him off that easy."

Miriam returned and they both stood there staring at the tree, with their hands on their hips. After about thirty seconds, there went his head again, peaking out. As soon as he spotted them, he quickly retreated behind the safety of the tree trunk. Miriam and Katie broke out laughing. They continued to stand still, waiting for the next sign of movement from behind the tree. This time, he did not pop his head around, even after two minutes had passed. They patiently waited.

"What's he going to do? Hide behind there all day?" Katie whispered.

"I don't know. Maybe so," she responded in a quiet voice.

"What do you think he would do if we walked up to him?" asked Katie.

"I don't know. Who would have ever thought he would run off the path and hide behind a tree? Who knows what he would do."

"Why don't we find out?" Katie mischievously suggested.

"I'm game," Miriam said with a smile.

"Go slowly," Katie whispered. "We don't want to ruin the surprise."

They slowly inched their way closer to the tree, cracking a few twigs along the way. As they approached nearer, his head suddenly appeared as he peaked around the corner of the tree trunk. When he saw they were off the path and heading in his direction, he took off running in the opposite direction deeper into the woods.

"Run," Katie yelled to Miriam. "Don't let him get away."

Miriam and Katie started chasing Vince through the woods. They ran and ran, with only their laughter slowing them down. They saw Vince slip, landing face down but he immediately leaped back up and continued to run. After a minute, there was a clearing with a parking lot and an apartment building on the other side of the lot. They looked around, but Vince was nowhere in sight.

"We've lost him," Katie said exhausted as she bent over and rested her hands on her knees.

"What were we going to do if we caught him?" inquired Miriam out of breath.

"I don't know. That's a good question."

Of course this made them laugh even harder.

"What do you think he thought we were going to do?" Katie asked.

"Who knows," Miriam laughed.

After regaining their breath, they turned around to go back through the forest. On their way back, they saw the spot where Vince had fallen.

"I thought we had him when he slipped," Katie laughed.

"I know. I've never seen anyone recover that quickly from a fall."

"Oh my gosh, look," Katie said as she pointed to the ground on the very spot Vince had fallen. "Is that Vince's?"

"That's his watch. I recognize it. He was wearing it the evening he was at my place. It was the one item he didn't remove."

Miriam reached down to pick it up.

"Don't," screamed Katie. Miriam looked at her with surprise. "Don't you see? It surrounded by poison ivy."

"He fell flat down in it. He must be covered with poison ivy."

At this they broke out laughing thinking about him falling face down in poison ivy with no shirt on and a pair of short shorts. They decided to cut the walk short and go back home and shower in case they had any poison ivy on themselves. Besides, they'd had more fun than expected. Their casual walk had ended up an adventure packed run.

As for Vince Well, there is a lesson to be learned. After all, the other squirrels in the forest know how to keep their nuts from getting into poison ivy.

THE AEROBIC STING—FEEL THE BURN

Katie had a friend named Betty who would call her every so often when she wanted to go to a singles function but did not want to go alone. It was Saturday night and the two of them had decided to attend a dance at a club in Georgetown. While at the party, Betty introduced an acquaintance of hers, Peter Findley, to Katie. Betty knew Peter was going to be attending and had talked about him before the party, describing Peter as, "Tall, handsome, intelligent and a true gentleman." Betty explained to Katie she had met Peter at a social gathering after work and they ran into each other a few more times at functions. She knew him well enough to say hello and have a short polite chat, and she really felt he was an extremely charming man who Katie should definitely get to know. They weren't at the party more than five minutes when Peter approached Betty for an introduction to her friend Katie.

Peter had a handlebar mustache that reminded Katie of a villain she had seen when she was a child watching Saturday morning cartoons. As he moved closer, the stench of cigarette smoke got stronger, almost becoming overbearing.

"Peter this is Katie. Katie, this is Peter," Betty said.

"So this is the Peter Findley you're always talking about," Katie said with a smile in Peter's direction.

"At your service," he responded as he bowed. "I can see why we were supposed to meet. You're perfect for me," he said as he took Katie's hand and kissed it softly.

Katie already didn't like something about him. He seemed to be full of himself. He smelled of a mixture of alcohol and tobacco. The mustache was a bit much for Katie. She wondered if he was trying to make some kind of statement.

"How old do you think I am?" he questioned Katie.

"I don't know."

"Come on, guess. Come on. How old?"

"I don't want to guess. That's a good way to get into trouble."

"Come on, I want you to."

Katie could tell he wasn't going to let it go so she studied his face. His face was hardened with deep lines, which Katie attributed to his cigarette smoking. Even though his eyes were beady, they were a beautiful bright blue. He looked early to mid sixties.

"Fifty-two," she kindly stated. The look on his face changed to a very serious frown and immediately changed back to a smile.

"You're teasing me. No really, how old do you think I am?"

"I don't know, just tell me."

"I'm forty-eight. People usually guess I'm a lot younger but I'm not. I'm forty-eight."

No wonder he frowned at first. Thank heavens she lied with her first guess. Katie and Peter politely talked for a minute and then Katie excused herself to go to the ladies room.

Later that evening Peter approached Katie and said, "Let's get out of here and get a drink. It'll be a good chance for us to get to know each other better."

"No thank you. I came to the party with Betty and I'm leaving with Betty."

"I've already checked with Betty and she said it would be all right for you to leave with me."

Katie walked off to find Betty.

Upon finding Betty, Katie discovered Peter mislead Betty by giving her the impression Katie wanted to leave with him. Katie was put off by Peter's bold lie and wondered, since it takes two to tango, how Peter thought he would be able to manipulate the situation to get her to leave with him. Either way, it just didn't matter. Katie told Betty she had no intention of leaving with Peter and there was something about him that made her uncomfortable.

Surprised, Betty said, "I can't believe you. First of all, he's good looking and second, he has so much charm and third, he's the President of a great investment company in D.C. You don't know a good thing when it's right in front of you."

That was obviously her opinion. Katie still visualized a villain who was tying the damsel in distress to the railroad tracks as the train was approaching. The villain would have lured the damsel into trusting him and then a second later, she finds herself trapped with no escape, as the train whistled its deathly approach. The word "smooth" came to Katie's mind.

"If he's so great, why don't you want him?"

"I don't know. He never seemed to be interested in me. We just ended up as friends. And besides, he seems perfect for you. Wasn't your father the President of a big investment company? You're always saying you wish you had someone like your father."

"You misunderstood me. I was talking about the quality of his character, not his job position."

"Well I think Peter's great. There are a lot of women who share my opinion too."

To Peter's disappointment, Katie left with Betty that night.

The next week Katie went with her girlfriend Laura to a private Superbowl party at a restaurant in Bethesda, Maryland. Laura and Katie got their food from the buffet line and searched for a table. A few minutes later, Katie looked up and saw Peter standing at their table with a plate of food.

"Katie, great to see you again. Do you mind if I join you?"

"No, I don't mind at all," she said feeling put on the spot.

"Laura, this is Peter. Peter this is Laura."

He leaned over and kissed Laura's hand as Laura blushed. Peter was very polite to both of them. Throughout the evening, Peter was jumping up and down bringing Laura and Katie drinks, deserts or anything he thought they might want that evening. Katie was impressed with how nice Peter was treating Laura. Laura was overweight and so many times in the past, shallow men would ignore Laura when they were talking, not even directing any conversation her way. Laura was obviously laughing and having a great time with Peter, which made Katie very happy.

Peter was very polite, charming and extremely attentive. Katie started to think perhaps she had misjudged him. Maybe he was a good guy. After all, she had nothing solid to base her negative feelings on except her gut first impression. Peter had an ego but he was a very successful man and a certain amount of ego must accompany success. Surely that wasn't enough to condemn a man. By the end of the night, Peter didn't seem like such a villain. Before leaving, Katie gave her phone number to Peter.

For their first date, Katie asked Peter if he would escort her to a concert of Livingston Taylor at Wolf Trap Barns since she had two free tickets.

Peter gladly agreed to go to the concert, which was on Thursday night. On the night of the concert, Peter greeted Katie at her door with a large bouquet of roses. Katie had previously told Peter she had a daughter named Samantha. Well, Peter didn't forget Samantha either, bringing her a large teddy bear.

During the concert Peter was so affectionate, gently holding Katie's hand as they listened to the music. After the concert Peter bought Katie a C.D. of Livingston Taylor. She liked that he opened the car door and really showed great manners. He gave her a respectable kiss on the cheek at the end of their date, which confirmed to Katie that Peter truly was a gentleman.

On their next date, they drove to Middleburg, Virginia, had lunch and walked around the small town. It was a lovely day and before they left Middleburg, Peter stopped in a little bakery and bought Katie and Samantha a big cream cheese and chocolate bar to take home for desert. Katie was at home by five o'clock. As Peter drove away, Katie was thinking how she was glad she had given Peter a chance. Of course she didn't care for his smoking but Peter made a conscious effort to only smoke outside and he never blew smoke in Katie's direction. He had even reduced the number of cigarettes he smoked daily. Katie hoped it would only be a matter of time before he would stop completely.

She was even starting to like his unique handlebar mustache. Instead of visualizing herself being tied to the train tracks, as he laughed an evil laugh, all the while twisting his handlebar mustache, she now saw herself being scooped up in his arms as he rescued her from any danger.

Every week, without exception, Peter would have flowers sent to Katie's home with a little note attached that said, "Thinking of you." He always signed the note, "Me" instead of Peter, which Katie thought was kind of cute. Katie and Peter saw each other practically every day for lunch, which was a nice break to her workday. He called her almost every evening just to say good night and to tell her he was thinking about her.

It became a routine for them to go out every Friday and Saturday night. Peter would find the nicest out of the way places to go. Katie enjoyed going to new locations. She had been to all the trendy hangouts and it was nice to get away from the usual crowd and do different things.

Within a few weeks, Peter and Katie changed their routine. They started spending all day Saturday together instead of Saturday evening. Peter liked to pick out a little town somewhere in the countryside and spend the day driving to it for an exploring adventure. They found some great little out of the way places to eat, plus it was fun walking around the towns, looking at the shops or checking out any bits of history in the area. Most of the time, Katie would be home before dinner, which gave her plenty of time to have dinner with Samantha, work on projects around the house, or do things with Samantha or her friends. It gave Peter time to spend with his children or at his office working.

Peter was a workaholic. His work ethic wasn't nine to five, Monday through Friday. He would go to the office to work on projects in the evenings and over the weekends too. Katie had never dated any man who put in such long hours seven days a week. He owned several rental properties too in addition to being very devoted to his three children. Not once had he missed a school event or game. Between both of their schedules, Katie was happy to have a quality day with him every Saturday. As a matter of fact, one of the things she liked about him was he wasn't needy and all time consuming. Over the past few months of dating each other, Katie felt it was great to be so secure that they didn't have to spend every moment together. Life seemed very balanced.

One day Katie met Peter at his apartment complex before they headed off for their out of town adventure. Suddenly, he looked out his window and in a panicked voice said, "Oh no! What's she doing here? She's never just dropped by like this."

"Who is it?"

"It's Nora."

"Who's Nora?"

"She's an old girlfriend."

"Really? How come this is the first time I've ever heard her name?"

"I don't know. I just don't feel the need to talk about her. The past is the past. I'm with you now."

"Why are you acting so panicked?"

"I'm not panicked. I just feel uncomfortable that she is dropping by."

"Don't worry about it. Just tell her you have plans and I'm sure she'll be embarrassed she dropped over without calling first. She'll probably never drop by again."

"You don't understand. She still isn't over me. I don't want to hurt her feelings or throw anything in her face. Please just be quiet. Don't let her know we're in here and she'll go away."

"This is ridiculous. We've been dating for months. Does she know you're seeing someone else?"

"No. I just never wanted to hurt her feelings."

"You're keeping her from moving on."

"Please, just be quiet. There's more to the story. I'll tell you as soon as she leaves. For now, please don't say a word. Just be quiet and I'll explain later. You've got to trust me."

Nora knocked at the door. Even though Katie didn't agree with Peter's way of handling the situation, she found herself standing perfectly still. They didn't make a sound. Nora knocked again, but after a moment, she left.

"It's sweet not to want to throw anything in Nora's face but you shouldn't hide our relationship. It isn't fair to Nora or me. Have you been staying in contact with her?"

"No. I've never called her but she continues to call me."

"How long ago did you two break up?"

"It's hard to say. I'm afraid in Nora's mind, we aren't broken up. I've tried to talk with her on several occasions but she never seems to accept it. She's very insecure and the thought of not having me in her life is devastating to her. She's older than me and I was never able to get past the age difference. I don't want to insult her and she is very sensitive about her age. Since you are younger, I just couldn't let her meet you. It would put her through too much trauma."

"Trauma? Really Peter. I think you're exaggerating."

"No. I'm sorry to say, I'm not."

"Well, that's sad. But she can't move on if you aren't telling her the truth. You don't need to let her know she is too old for you, but you do need to let her know you have moved on and have someone else."

"Maybe your right. I'll take care of it."

Peter's words did not comfort Katie. She doubted he was telling her the complete truth. The panicked look on his face when he saw Nora through the window didn't seem to fit the scenario.

"Let's have a nice day and no more talk of Nora," said Peter.

When they left, there was an envelope taped to his front door. Peter did not show Katie the note Nora wrote but Nora had left some tootsie rolls in the envelope that Peter shared with Katie.

The next weekend, Jasmine was having a party at her house. It would be the perfect opportunity for Peter to meet Katie's friends. In all the months they had been dating, Peter had not met any of Katie's friends and she hadn't met any of his. Peter claimed it was because he was selfish and didn't want to share her. Katie was flattered, but felt an important part of dating is meeting friends. Peter agreed to remedy the situation.

On the night of Jasmine's party, Peter called. "I'm so sorry but my son has a game. I'll have to miss Jasmine's party. You go ahead and have a nice time."

"Why don't you swing by after the game? The party will go until late."

"No can do. We have plans to go out for a late dinner after the game. It's bonding time."

Even though Katie was disappointed, she appreciated he was so involved with his son. After all, she certainly understood, being a parent herself.

When Katie was with Peter, she felt as if she were the only woman on the face of the earth and that he was a very loving, attentive man. However, lately, when she was away from him, she found herself having doubts about their relationship.

Peter still called Katie every so often in the evenings to wish her a good night. He still took her to lunch once in a while, and not a single week had gone by since they met that he hadn't sent her flowers, always signing the card, "Me." However, Peter had not made time to meet any of her best friends. He was either consumed with responsibilities at his job or the latest reason they couldn't see each other was because he was baby-sitting his children for his ex-wife Margaret, so she could go out on dates.

Katie's girlfriend Meg and her husband had a party and Katie found herself, once again, going alone while Peter babysat his children. This was the second Saturday night in a row for him to baby-sit. Mind you, these were not small children, these were teenagers. It didn't seem natural that his teenage children wouldn't have a life of their own. Katie agreed it was important for parents to keep a watchful eye on children, especially during the teenage years, but she wondered why his teenagers didn't want to spend time with their own friends on Saturday night instead of always preferring to stay at home and watch a movie with their Dad. After all, they saw him all the time.

Katie and her teenage daughter Samantha had a very close relationship, but Katie knew Samantha would much rather be spending time with her friends on the weekends rather than watching television or movies with her Mom.

Even though Peter always had a reason why they couldn't get together, Katie doubted him more and more. Peter seemed to be explaining himself too much. Another thing he had recently started doing was making plans with her and then canceling them at the last minute. Things just didn't seem the same, which made Katie wondered if there was another woman in the picture, and if that woman was Nora.

One day, Katie confronted Peter about her anxiety.

"I never knew you were so insecure. I thought you understood I have many obligations in my life. You can't always be the center of attention Katie. I hate it when women are needy," he emphasized.

Katie didn't press Peter further. She had always felt she was not the type to be insecure. However, she had learned from past experiences whenever she felt insecure in a relationship, it was because the man was doing something to make her feel that way. Katie felt any doubtful feelings were not due to an inadequacy of hers, but were due to her picking up vibes given by the other party. She had a sinking feeling there was a reason she was not feeling good about Peter Findley.

The next weekend, Jasmine asked Katie if she and Peter could come over on Friday or Saturday for some wine and cheese on her patio. Katie really wanted Peter and Jasmine to meet.

"Please come meet Jasmine."

"Sorry, baby. I just can't. I'm going to Margaret's to baby-sit again. She has a date."

"You've got two in high school and one in junior high. I don't understand why you must baby-sit. They are old enough to be on their own. Plus, it's not like you don't ever see them. You see them all the time."

"Katie, you've got to stop being jealous of my children."

"I'm not jealous. I just want you to go to Jasmine's house with me."

"I can't. I'm with my kids."

"Both Friday and Saturday?"

"I'm sorry baby. I've already obligated myself."

"Well unobligate yourself. You have an obligation to me too. I'm your girlfriend. Certainly that has to count for something."

"I can see your point. I understand why you are upset."

"Great! Then do something about it. And, why would your ex-wife want you at her house when her date shows up. Isn't that uncomfortable for both of you?"

"Not at all. Come on baby, be a sport. You know I love spending time with you. I just can't do it Friday or Saturday evening."

"What's with this baby stuff? Why do you call me baby all the time? You use to use my name. For the last month, you've called me baby. My name is Katie."

"I just can't do anything right."

"I don't like being called baby, it's too generic."

As Katie spoke those words, she felt ill. She knew many times when a man replaces your name with a generic name, it is to help keep him out of trouble by reducing the chance of him slipping up and saying the wrong name. Now she did not believe every man who uses a term of endearment is doing it for that reason. Most of the time it truly is a term of endearment, nothing more. But in certain cases, it's done to help keep the unfaithful man from getting himself into trouble. Life is a lot easier if all the women you date at the same time are referred to as "Baby." Katie was positive Peter had stopped using her name for that reason.

Katie was exhausted from debating with Peter and knew their conversation was going nowhere.

"Okay snookums, you get your way. We won't go to Jasmines."

"Snookums? Don't call me that."

"If I'm baby, you can be snookums."

"I don't mind you calling me a sweet name but don't have it be snookums."

"Nope. It's my call."

"Okay, okay. You've made your point. What do you want me to call you?"

Exasperated she yelled, "How about Katie!"

"Fine."

"Thank you. Now, what about Jasmine's? Will you see if you can work something out?"

"You're adamant about this, aren't you?"

"Yes. You've done this to me too many times."

"Who's going to be at Jasmine's?"

"Just Jasmine and her boyfriend."

"What's her boyfriend's name?"

"Ivan. Why?"

"I just wanted to know everyone who would be there."

"I told you, just Jasmine and Ivan. Why? Does it matter?"

"Not at all. I guess you're right. I'm not being fair to you baby, I mean Katie. I'll tell you what, tell Jasmine Friday night is fine with me. I'll figure something out."

"Thanks."

"Feel better now?"

"Yes," she responded not really feeling that much better. Katie was now wondering why he needed to know who was going to be at Jasmine's. Who was he afraid of running into?

When Friday night rolled around, Peter and Katie headed for Jasmine's.

Nestled in the back of a cul-de-sac, Jasmine's house had a cozy charm that reminded Katie of a house in a childhood storybook. It was a cottage home with rustic shutters around the pained windows and flower boxes filled with beautiful coral flowers under each window. Gingerbread scrollwork made beautiful trim, which added to the cottage allure. Even though there was traffic whizzing by only a few blocks away, Jasmine's enchanted property made you forget.

Jasmine greeted Peter and Katie at the screen door and guided them through her home to reach the backyard. As they walked through Jasmine's home, they could see antique pots and pans surrounding the hearth. Her place had an inviting, unpretentious appeal that said, "Kick your shoes off and relax."

Once outside, Katie could tell Peter was taken aback with Jasmine's landscaping, which was her pride and joy.

"This place is a little paradise," Peter exclaimed. "I can see why Katie says your backyard is one of her favorite places to visit."

You could tell Jasmine spent hours daily tending her plants and flowers. Candles and lanterns were scattered throughout her garden, which gave her backyard a warm romantic glow. The fragrant deep purple flowers of lavender were everywhere and Jasmine had butterfly bushes, lilies, marigolds, sunflowers, hollyhocks, black-eyed Susans, hibiscus and daisies. Hedges surrounded the property as a living fence.

In the back of the garden, Ivan was standing under an arbor that was covered in pink roses. He greeted Peter and Katie with a warm smile. Ivan was a slow talking, down to earth flannel shirt and jeans type of guy who was also a nature lover, just like Jasmine. Ivan stood over six feet tall, had broad shoulders and possessed the kind of handsome rugged appearance that made every women look twice. And to top it off, he was a nice man and an interesting man. If Ivan and Jasmine weren't gardening, they were off at Ivan's lakeside cabin canoeing or fishing off his boat, hiking in the woods or off on one of their many vacations soaking up the local culture to whichever exotic destination they had chosen. Ivan and Jasmine were both very happy and comfortable in their relationship. Katie really liked Ivan and found him a great improvement over Jasmine's last boyfriend, Ralph.

After a full tour of the garden, Jasmine escorted everyone back to the patio table for drinks. Jasmine's black cast iron table was covered with a light lavender tablecloth. A blue pottery platter was placed in the middle of the table, which had Brie cheese, crackers and grapes adorning the center. There was also a platter of shrimp. She had a bottle of wine and four crystal glasses set out.

"Now that's what I could use. A nice glass of wine," Peter said.

After Ivan poured the wine, he lifted his glass and said, "To a fun evening with good food and great friends. We welcome you Peter, to our little group."

"Here, here," everyone responded.

"Thank you. It's nice to be here enjoying all of you with this marvelous cabernet sauvignon. Wine is wonderful. Everything gets better with wine."

"Women get prettier," said Katie.

"And thinner," added Jasmine.

"At least until the next morning," laughed Katie.

"Men get smarter," said Ivan.

"I'd better drink up. There's no time to waste," joked Peter.

Ivan takes another sip of his wine, "I'm feeling smarter already."

"Did you know there is a wine called Fat Bastard?" said Jasmine.

"Yes. I've heard of it but haven't tasted it yet," answered Peter.

Jasmine continued, "There's also one called Naked Lady."

"Now that I've had," laughed Peter. "Here's to naked ladies."

"Here's to naked ladies," repeated Ivan as he lifted his glass.

"I have a feeling we aren't talking about wine anymore," said Katie.

"I hope not," Peter laughed.

"That's what I thought. You guys are terrible," Katie said as she gave Peter a quick kiss on the cheek.

"Better a naked lady than a fat bastard," laughed Ivan.

Peter picks up a piece of shrimp and puts it in his mouth. "Oh!"

"What is it Peter?" asked Katie.

"I was laughing and not paying attention. I put the tail in first."

"I thought you liked tail," teased Katie.

"Better have more wine Peter. You need to be smarter. You don't know one end from the other," said Ivan.

"Now that's a different story I'd rather not share," Peter said as he looked downward as if in shame. "Don't judge me."

"Are we back to fat bastards?" Jasmine said as everyone broke out in laughter.

"Ouch!" Peter laughed. "I set myself up for that comment. I want to go back to the original toast. To naked ladies!"

The evening turned out to be relaxing and yet filled with laughter. Everyone seemed to be on a roll with humorous banter. By the end of the night, Peter told Katie he was sorry he had missed Jasmine's other parties. He said he really enjoyed meeting her best friend and he could see why Katie thought so much of Jasmine.

On Saturday, Peter and Katie did not make plans to see each other. Peter was with his children and Katie needed the day to take Samantha shopping for new shoes. Katie was once again feeling great about her relationship with Peter. A relaxing evening in Jasmine's beautiful garden was just what they had both needed.

During the week, Peter and Katie made plans to spend Saturday afternoon exploring another little town. On Thursday night, Katie received a call from her neighbor, Susie Murphy. They were having a few couples over for a barbecue on Saturday afternoon and asked if Peter and Katie would like to join them in the festivities.

Katie said yes. After all, she and Peter could explore the towns anytime. This would be a good opportunity for them to spend time with other couples. Katie wanted Peter to meet the Murphy family. Since Samantha and Katie had no family in Virginia, they considered the Murphy's the closest people they had to a family.

On Friday night Peter called, "Ready to take an afternoon tomorrow and explore another town? I found a new one I'd like to check out," he said with enthusiasm.

"That would be great but we've been invited to an afternoon barbecue with the Murphy family. I've been talking about them forever and now is a great chance for all of you to meet."

"I can't. Margaret wants me to baby-sit again."

"This is an afternoon barbecue, not an evening event. We can go to the barbeque and then you can still baby-sit that evening. We don't have to stay long."

"I can't. She wants me over there early."

"What time? Like I said, you can do both."

"Look, I don't like being rushed. I need to watch the kids and I don't want to have to worry about watching the clock. I'd rather meet them sometime when I don't have to be somewhere else."

"Just a minute ago we were going to go exploring. Now all of a sudden you can't?"

"I wasn't thinking clearly. We really wouldn't have had much time to run around. I totally forgot until now that she wanted me over there early."

Katie felt sick. She knew he wasn't telling her the truth.

Later that week, Katie got the usual flowers from Peter. When he first started sending her flowers and signing the card with "Me," she thought it was cute. But when she opened the card from him and once again saw it was signed with "Me," she now found it suspicious. She was positive it was his way of not leaving evidence that he had any involvement with her. She wondered how many other, "Me's" he had sent out to females.

For the first time, Katie and Peter did not have plans to see each other over the weekend. She knew in her heart things had changed. She wasn't sure she wanted to pursue this relationship anymore. And yet, she didn't want to let go. What if she were wrong? What if Peter really was working, spending time with his children, and truly being faithful to her? Could she chance walking away on just a gut feeling? She missed the way she used to feel with Peter.

On Sunday morning, Peter called and asked if he could take her to brunch. Katie was glad he called because she had really missed him over the weekend.

Within the hour, Peter picked Katie up and they drove to a restaurant in Old Town Alexandria. Peter requested a nice quiet romantic table in the back. As they followed the maitre d' to the table, they passed a man and women who were sitting at a booth. Once the couple spotted Peter, they both called out his name.

"Peter, Peter, over here."

Peter kept walking. They called out his name again but Peter showed no response.

Katie announced, "Peter, those people are speaking to you."

Peter looked over his shoulder and responded, "I'll come back."

Katie observed that Peter seemed tremendously uncomfortable with seeing them. He had that same nervous look on his face the day Nora showed up at his apartment.

Peter firmly held Katie's elbow, leading her at a quick pace to the table. After they were seated, Peter told Katie he needed to talk with the couple who had flagged him down. He said he was doing some private business with them and would Katie mind waiting until the waiter came and giving him their order. Peter instructed Katie to order him black coffee and a western omelet. He then got up and went to the table where the other couple was sitting.

After the waiter took their order, Katie decided to see what was going on since Peter was still visiting with the other couple. As she approached the table, she could hear him saying, "Again, I'm so sorry. This is really embarrassing, that's why I just had to explain so you wouldn't have the wrong idea."

Just then, the couple spotted Katie and quickly said to Peter, "Here she comes now."

At that point, Katie was at their table, but Peter grabbed Katie forcefully by the arm and said, "We have to go now. It was nice seeing you."

When Peter and Katie got back to their table, Katie questioned Peter about what had just happened.

"I heard you apologize saying you were so embarrassed. What were you embarrassed about?"

"I don't know what you're talking about."

"Yes you do."

"No I don't. I told you they were business acquaintances and we had to straighten up a few matters."

"Why didn't you introduce me?"

"I'm sorry baby, I wasn't thinking."

"It sounded as if you were talking about me."

"You? We weren't talking about you. Come on baby, let's have a nice brunch. Stop this nonsense."

Katie found herself exhausted from this exchange and sat in silence. She felt her energy draining from her body.

After Katie returned home, she thought about her relationship with Peter. She had gone from feeling on top of the world, to feeling insecure and unsure. Katie wasn't enjoying herself anymore. She wasn't ready to walk away from Peter but she felt more and more miserable about the way things had changed.

That week Katie got the usual flowers signed with what she was now calling the, "no evidence" signature of, "Me."

On Thursday night Peter phoned. Before he could say anything, Katie told him she was going to the movies with Jasmine on Friday night and Samantha was having a slumber party at her house on Saturday, both of which were lies. Katie felt she needed a break from Peter to gain some perspective.

On Saturday evening Peter called from his cell phone and said since he knew Katie was already booked for the weekend, he had obligated himself to baby-sit with his children again while Margaret went out on another date. Peter said he needed to get off his cell phone because he was pulling into Margaret's driveway. He had made plans with his children to watch a movie, which he had rented earlier in the day. He continued to say he was spending the night over at Margaret's because Margaret was staying overnight with her boyfriend. Peter said he would call Katie sometime Sunday afternoon and maybe they could get together for dinner that evening.

Katie told him that would be great, but in reality, she knew they would never make it to dinner. Peter's phone call made her realize it was time to find a way to check out his story. Katie pulled out the phone book and found Margaret's phone number. She was thankful it wasn't unlisted. She saw the street address where Margaret lived and recognized the name of the street. Katie had once gone to a baby shower in that neighborhood, which was a lovely wooded addition with large homes.

After a couple of hours, Katie decided to call. She had purposely waited a couple of hours to insure that if by any slim chance Peter was telling the truth and Margaret actually had a date, then Margaret would be on her date and out of the house.

Katie's hands were shaking as she dialed the phone.

"Hello," said the woman who answered the phone.

"Hi. Is Peter Findley there?"

"Who is this?"

"This is a friend of his. My name's Katie. Who is this?"

"Margaret," she replied in an irritated tone. "How did you get this number?"

"I looked it up in the phone book."

"What are you calling here for? Why don't you call him at his apartment?"

"Peter told me he was baby-sitting for you tonight."

"Baby-sitting who?"

"Your children."

"That's absurd. They're teenagers. They don't need a baby-sitter."

"He told me he was baby-sitting while you went out on a date."

"A date? I'm not dating anyone."

"I'm so sorry, I must have misunderstood."

"I'm sure you didn't. I'm sure that's exactly what he told you. For your information, Peter has very little contact with his children. I resent that he's using them as his excuse. Don't ever call here again. I don't want to be involved in any of this," Margaret said as she slammed down the receiver.

Well, Katie had her answer. Peter was lying. She imagined Nora was the woman he was seeing. How foolish she had been.

About ten minutes later the phone rang, it was Peter.

"Why did you call Margaret? What in the world is wrong with you?"

"I was calling to talk with you. After all, you said you would be there."

"I know but you shouldn't have called. It upset her terribly and it's rude to throw another women in her face. I've been trying to protect her from this. After all, she is the mother of my children! You had no business calling her."

"I wasn't calling her. I thought she would be on her date. I was going by what you told me."

"I can't take much more of this Katie. And why in the world would you have called her home number? Why didn't you call my cell? You are totally out of line baby. Totally out of line."

"Peter, Margaret told me she isn't dating anyone. She told me you don't baby-sit and barely see your children."

"Of course she told you that. She's mad and trying to cause trouble."

"Where are you?"

"I took the kids out for ice cream because Margaret's date was late. That's why she was still there. Her date had car trouble but said he'd be by later. When I found out I decided it would be best to get out of the house and treat the kids to some ice cream. There was no need to hang around and wait for her date to show. Then I get this hysterical phone call from her because of your call."

Still not believing him she pushed him further, "Great. So I'll call you there later, after I know she's gone."

"No. This is my time with the kids. Listen baby, I've got to run but I'll see you tomorrow. I'll give you all the attention you can stand but please, stop this madness. No more phone calls. Okay?"

"Okay," she replied out of habit.

She wondered if she had turned into a crazy, jealous person? She needed proof of her own sanity.

Later that night, the phone rang and it was Peter calling from his cell phone. Katie could tell he was standing outside. She could hear cars zooming by in the background, which indicated to her that he was on a busy street, not a quiet residential neighborhood. When she asked him where he was calling from, he replied he was standing in Margaret's backyard. He said he wanted to talk without eavesdropping ears. Katie could hear Peter exhaling from his cigarette. Peter said he and the kids had watched a movie earlier and the kids were now in bed. Peter said he was getting ready to go to bed too. Finally, a statement that was probably true.

Katie hung up the phone, realizing she couldn't stand not knowing the truth any longer. If she was ever going to be able to walk away from Peter, she had to confirm her suspicions were true. She needed to know if she was so screwed up that she needed counseling or was he the true villain, ready to tie her to the tracks and let the train flatten her.

Katie wrote down Margaret's address and drove to her house. After all, according to Peter, Margaret was gone for the weekend and Peter said the kids were in bed. When Katie arrived, she noticed Margaret's garage door was open. There were two cars in the garage. There was no sign of Peter's car parked in the garage or on the street. Katie could see a woman through a small front window of what looked to be the kitchen. She suspected that was Margaret. Next she drove to Peter's apartment and his car was not there either. Since Katie didn't know Nora's last name or where she lived, there was no way to verify if Peter was at Nora's, so she drove back home.

The next day, Peter showed up unannounced on her doorstep. Katie told Peter she did not appreciate him stopping by without calling. He immediately turned around, went to his car and called Katie from his cell phone. In the beginning of their relationship, she might have thought that was cute, but the cuteness had worn off. She didn't take the call.

A moment later, Peter was at the door, ringing the bell so Katie walked outside to talk with Peter. As she got closer, she could smell alcohol on his breath.

"I'm sorry I didn't call first. I just missed you so much this weekend," he said as he puffed on his cigarette.

"How was your evening, Peter?"

"It was great. Listen, I forgive you for calling Margaret. I know you just acted crazy out of love for me. Now that you know never to do that again, everything is fine."

"I know what you did last night and I don't want to hear anymore lies," Katie said firmly.

"What are you talking about? You know I was with my kids."

"No you weren't."

"Oh baby, you've got to stop this."

"If you want to stand a chance with me at all, you won't tell me one more lie. In all fairness, I should tell you that it's a small world and I happen to have a couple of friends who know you and your female friend. They told me who you were with. If you lie in anyway about this, I'll never see you again. It will be over for good. If you tell the truth, we'll stand a chance of working this out. It's your call. Honesty or a lie. You determine our future."

Katie was shocked to discover her bluff worked. Peter quickly stated, "Okay. Okay. Let me explain. I admit I saw Nora. I didn't want to upset you by telling you the truth. I was just trying to let Nora down easily."

"And did you?"

"Well, it wasn't easy but I made great progress."

"Great progress?"

"Yes. You'd be proud of me baby. I realized you were right. Nora needed to know I had moved on. I had to set the record straight for the sake of our relationship"

"So you went out with her for me?"

"No. Of course not. I went out with her for us. I only lied because I didn't want to jeopardize what we have with the truth."

In Katie's mind, that pretty much said it all.

"I'm so sorry Katie. I never meant to hurt you."

"Don't you mean you never meant to get caught?"

"That too," he honestly admitted. "It feels great to get all this off my chest. It's been a terrible burden."

"So, when are you seeing Nora next?" Katie asked calmly.

"Now that we are being totally honest, I have to tell you. Nora asked me months ago to attend a concert with her. These were previous plans we made and I just can't leave her hanging with no escort on such short notice. She's already bought the tickets."

"Okay. That's fine with me."

"You're a doll baby. An absolute doll." Peter kissed Katie's hand.

"How long do you think it will take to let Nora down gently?"

"Three months. Just give me three more months and then we can work on us."

"Actually, I don't think three months is enough for a fragile person such as Nora. I think I'm going to give you and Nora a lot more time. As a matter of fact, I think the two of you need exclusive time together."

Katie headed for her front door.

"Wait. What are you talking about? Are you upset?"

"No Peter, not at all. As a matter of fact, I want to thank you. You've just made everything so much easier."

By now, Peter was sensing things weren't quite as he thought. "Wait baby. You said if I told the truth, we'd stand a chance of working this out. That's the only reason why I chose honesty. You tricked me. You said we could work this out!"

As Katie was shutting the front door, she stopped long enough to look at Peter and respond, "I lied."

She had been thrown on the train tracks and injured but she would survive.

Several months later, Katie was sitting on her small patio when Peter stopped by unannounced. Katie immediately got up, planning on going inside but Peter intercepted, holding his hand on the door. "Please just give me one minute with you," he pleaded. "Please Katie. Can't you just give me one minute?"

She was surprised she didn't feel angry with him. Conveniently for Peter, time had helped heal her memory.

"Look, I don't blame you for being upset with me. I'm the first to admit I've made plenty of mistakes in the past. But what I don't want to have happen is to be punished for the rest of my life because of my own stupidity. I don't want the best thing that has ever happened to me to slip away."

"It doesn't matter anymore."

"I didn't treat you the way I should have. You deserve so much more and I want to prove to you I'm a changed man. I was thinking the other day about how much fun we always had together. What you and I had was something people look for everyday and it doesn't come along but once in a blue moon. Don't throw all of this away. Give me a chance to win you back. To spoil you. To prove to you I'm worthy of your love. Please Katie. That's all I'm asking."

"I'm over you, Peter."

"You can't mean that. Look what I bought." He reached in his pocket and pulled out a locket. "Do you remember this locket? We saw it in an antique store one day. You said it was just like the one your Grandmother wore and you said it brought back great memories."

Katie looked at the locket, remembering the day she saw it in the store window. It had been the most perfect day with Peter. It reminded her of how happy they had been.

"Take it. Please Katie. I want you to have it since it brought you fond memories of your Grandmother."

Katie took the locket. She was surprised to find there was no reluctance on her part. She was touched by his gesture. The thing that upset Katie the most was that even though she had lost faith in Peter, she hated to admit it but at that very moment, as she held the locket in her hand and listened to him talk about how much he missed her, she found herself attracted to him again. They had always had chemistry so she knew it was dangerous to be listening to his smooth, charming talk. Visions of their past kisses started creeping into her head.

Sooner than she would like to admit, she found herself thinking maybe it could be different this time. After all, everyone deserves a second chance. The Peter trance had taken over.

Peter said he had to check on some rental houses in Bethesda, Maryland and wanted to know if Katie could meet him for dinner later that day.

Katie agreed, but the moment she shut the door behind him, she snapped out of her trance. His spell was broken. What was wrong with her? She desperately needed her head examined. What was it about Peter that made her abandon her sanity? If he wasn't honest with her the first time, why should she expect him to be honest with her the second time? Well, she would just have to leave him a message on his apartment voice mail before he returned home. She would tell him she just couldn't see him and she would get herself out of this dinner date. But then she knew he would still feel a victory. He would know she caved once and he would think through persistence, he could charm her again. She didn't have the confidence to assure herself she wouldn't let that happen. She needed this man out of her life, once and for all; maybe.

Katie decided to go to dinner, but this time, she had a plan to give herself a little protection.

Katie immediately picked up the phone and dialed Miriam. Miriam happened to live a few blocks from the restaurant where Katie had agreed to meet Peter for dinner. Luckily, Miriam was home and ready to assist.

Peter and Katie were supposed to meet inside the restaurant at seven o'clock. Katie drove to Miriam's house and called Peter's cell phone, using her own cell phone. It was now around six-fifty and Katie knew Peter would already be at the restaurant eagerly awaiting her arrival. Katie informed him she was running late and was so sorry but it would be more like seven-thirty or eight before she could make it. She asked if he would please wait for her, which he kindly agreed to, telling Katie to take her time because she was well worth the wait.

After Katie's phone call, Miriam followed Katie in her car to the restaurant. It was seven fifteen when Miriam proceeded to the restaurant. Katie sat patiently waiting in the parking garage.

At seven-forty, Katie walked into the restaurant. She had originally planned on waiting longer but couldn't stand sitting in the garage a second more. She just had to know how things with Peter and Miriam were going and if Peter had taken the bait. She saw Peter talking to Miriam at the bar. She waved at Peter to get his attention.

Peter jumped up from the bar and came over with the biggest grin on his face. He gave Katie a long hug and a quick kiss on the cheek.

"You look beautiful tonight. Oh, baby, I'm so glad you're here."

The maitre d' escorted them to their table, which was in a dark corner in the back. The glow of the flickering candlelight gave the table a romantic feel.

Peter took Katie's hand and whispered as he leaned across the table, "Everything is going to be different now darling. From this point on, it's just you and me. I'm ready to work on us now." As he kissed her hand he muttered, "I love you baby. You're the one. It's our time darling. Our time for happiness." He continued thoughtfully, "There is only a happy future for both of us now. The worst is behind us. I need you to forgive me Katie. Will you do that for me?"

"Yes," Katie found herself reply.

"Oh baby, I'm the happiest man in the world. I couldn't have gone another day without hearing your sweet voice. Life is too short. We shouldn't waste another moment apart."

Katie felt her heart melt.

"I'm ready to devote myself to making you happy. That's all I want is your happiness. Will you let me give you that?"

"Yes," Katie softly agreed.

"Baby, you won't regret it."

"One thing Peter."

"Anything. Just name it."

"I want a monogamous relationship with an honest man who loves and respects me. Can you promise me I'll have that?"

Peter responded, "You deserve that and I'm going to give it to you." He continued, "I could spend the whole night just looking into your eyes and that would be enough for me. I want to put one hundred and ten percent into us."

Katie found his words soothing and at that moment, Katie felt no fear. She knew in her heart Peter was telling her the truth. She knew as she looked into his blue eyes, her future would be filled with wonderful times. She felt happier than she had been in a long time. He was not the villain. There was no train coming down the tracts to run her over. She was safe again.

Katie asked Peter to order her a drink and told him she'd be right back. She just had to go to the ladies powder room, which was her designated meeting place with Miriam. Although she now felt a little guilty she had asked Miriam to assist her in testing Peter's honesty. After all, it was obvious Peter was ready to, as he said, "work on us."

As Katie neared the bathroom her, "Peter trance" began wearing off and her insecure feelings were reappearing. She swung open the bathroom door, anxious to hear Miriam's take on her future with Peter.

"Oh, Miriam, if I didn't know better, I'd think he really cares."

Miriam started laughing, "Oh he cares all right. He cares about himself."

Katie thought she heard a train whistle in the distance.

Miriam then proceeded to tell Katie the events that took place with her and Peter before Katie's arrival.

Miriam said as soon as she entered the restaurant, she immediately spotted Peter sitting at the bar. Of course Katie had shown Miriam pictures of him, which probably weren't necessary because his long handlebar mustache stood out. Katie had told Miriam to look in the bar area for Peter. She knew he would be there enjoying his Crown Royal.

Miriam stated she pulled some bubble gum, which was conveniently left in her purse from when her niece was visiting, out of her purse and into her mouth to help her get into character. She walked up to Peter and said in a cutesy way, "You're the most attractive man in this bar. May I have a seat?"

"By all means." Standing up he pulled out the bar stool for her.

"What's your name?" Miriam asked as she snapped her bubble gum.

"Peter, Peter Findley. And what's your name lovely lady?"

Blushing, Miriam answered "Abigail."

"Abigail. What a lovely name."

"Thank you. It's after Grammy Abby," she replied in her best fake cutesy voice.

"And what do you do for a living Abigail?"

"I'm an aerobics instructor," she lied.

Miriam said she could see the pleased look on Peter's face. She was sure he was visualizing her in different positions.

"An aerobics instructor. I should have guessed. You have the most beautiful body."

"I know," she said while blowing a big bubble with her pink gum. "I get that a lot."

"I'm sure you do."

"What do you do for a living? I bet you're something important. I can always tell that about a guy. Ya know, with your wearing a suit and all."

"I'm the President of Washington Fidelity Assessment Company."

"Wow. A president! That's impressive."

"Being an aerobics instructor is pretty impressive too."

"Thanks, but it's not as impressive as being a President. Do you get to go to the White House? You know, being a President and all," she said with a serious voice and big innocent eyes.

Peter laughed, "You're refreshing Abigail. I think you and I are going to get along just fine."

"Wow, I wish I were a President. I'm the most flexible of all the aerobics instructors. That has to count for something."

"It sure does." Peter was beaming with anticipation. "Aerobics instructors keep the world healthy and I must say you are the most gorgeous aerobics instructor I've ever seen."

"Thanks. I have one of the most popular classes."

"I bet you do."

The bartender asked Miriam what she wanted and she replied "Something frozen. Do you have any umbrellas? I just love umbrellas in drinks. They're so cute." She was doing a great job keeping up her dumb girly routine and Peter's ego was too big to see the truth. Peter couldn't see beyond his new goal of getting it on with an alleged aerobics instructor.

When the bartender brought her drink, Peter quickly said, "Put it on my tab."

"Wow. Thanks."

"My pleasure. It's not very often I have the chance to buy a beautiful aerobics instructor like yourself a drink."

"It's not very often I get a man as handsome as you to buy me a drink."

"I find that hard to believe. I'd think you have men all over you."

"Oh, I do. It's just that I'm usually not that attracted to them. You're not like other men. You have an air of importance. It must be that President thing."

"You are a refreshing jewel. I really get a kick out of you," Peter said smiling.

Miriam blew a big pink bubble that popped on her face. "You should see how big I can blow."

"I'd love to see that." His mind was racing with ideas that did not relate to bubble gum.

"No one can beat me at blowing. I'm the best."

By now Peter was ecstatic. He could barely contain his excitement at his new future conquest. His imagination was not letting him down.

"Abigail, you have the loveliest eyes. I could stare into your eyes all evening. I bet you get that from a lot of men."

"Not really. I get them from my Mother."

"Listen Abigail, do you have any plans for the weekend?"

"Not really."

"I was wondering if you'd like to go away with me. I've always wanted to check out the sunset in Annapolis. Would you like to see a beautiful sunset in Annapolis this weekend?"

"Annapolis? What state is that in?"

"Why it's right here in the state of Maryland."

"Wow. I didn't know that. You're really smart aren't you?"

Laughing Peter said, "I'd love to teach you what I know."

"That's nice of ya," she said while smacking her gum.

"There are some really great places to eat in Annapolis. Do you like crab cakes?"

"Chocolate cake's my favorite," she innocently said with a serious expression.

He laughed, "I think I can manage finding you some chocolate cake. How about it?"

"Well, I don't know ya very well."

"What better way to get to know me? We'll be able to spend quality time together. We could drive to Annapolis, spend the day, have a nice dinner and try out this new bed and breakfast I've heard is fantastic."

"I've never had breakfast in bed. I've had a lot in bed, but not breakfast."

Peter could hardly hold back his excitement. "We'll have a great time. What do ya say? Please? You won't regret it."

"How long does it take to get to Annapolis? Can we get there in a day?"

Laughing he replied, "Of course we can. I'll make sure we get there in time for a nice dinner with a view of the sunset. It's the most beautiful sunset you'll ever see. I wouldn't want you to miss it. Just picture this scene. You and I, holding hands as we watch the most brilliant orange sunset reflecting off the water. You can't get a sunset like that around here."

"It does sound kinda nice."

"Of course it's nice. How about it Abigail? Will you let me show you a wonderful time? I'll make sure you have the best chocolate cake around."

"I do love chocolate cake. Especially chocolate layer cake."

"Yes. That's what they specialize in is chocolate lay her, I mean layer cake. You won't regret it. Come on baby. What do you say?"

"Well, okay."

"Great! Now that that's settled, I have to tell you something because I really want to be honest with you. I'm meeting an old girlfriend here tonight. We broke up months ago but she's still hanging on. She needs to get closure in order to move on so I agreed to meet her. When she comes in, I'll have to go but in no way do I want you to misinterpret any of this. This is strictly for me to allow her closure."

"What if she wants you back?"

"She already knows that's not going to happen. She just had a few things she wanted to say and I never gave her the chance. If this helps her move on with her life then it's worth it. The thing is, I don't want to throw a beautiful aerobics instructor in her face. You understand don't you?"

"I guess."

"Can I have your phone number, Abigail?"

"I don't have one. I just moved and I haven't put the phone in yet."

"Okay. What about your cell?"

"I don't own a cell."

"Where do you teach aerobics? I'll call you there."

"I'm off work for the next two weeks. Ya know, because I was moving."

"All right baby. You call me at my office and we'll get the details settled. I need to know where to pick you up. Can you do that? Will you call me?"

"Okay. Give me your business card."

Just then Katie walked in and Peter spotted her. "That's her. I don't want her to see me giving you my card."

"How will I know your number?"

"It's in the phone book. Peter Findley of Washington Fidelity Assessment Company in Washington, D.C. Can you remember that?"

She played with him. "Peter Fidelity of Washington Findley Assessment Company."

"No. Peter Findley of Washington Fidelity."

"It's confusing. Too many things that sound alike."

Peter was now getting frustrated. "Listen Abigail. Peter Findley of Washington Fidelity Assessment Company."

"Peter Fidelity of Fidelity Company?"

"No, just call the Washington Fidelity Assessment Firm. They'll know who I am."

"You've got me all confused now."

Frustrated he said, "Look, here's my business card." He pulls out his card and slips it under a napkin. "Now take the card from under the napkin after I leave. Call me this week. You promise you'll call me?"

"I will. I promise."

"Good girl. You've made my evening, doll. Now call me. We'll have a great time. I'm going to spoil you rotten."

"Okay, I'd like that," she replied while snapping her gum.

Katie had heard enough. She found herself feeling furious with Peter.

Miriam started imitating some of Peter's past known lines to Katie, "Oh baby, you have the most beautiful eyes." Miriam picked up Katie's hand and kissed it.

All of a sudden Katie found herself laughing because the whole situation seemed comical. "Can you believe this? Thank you so much Miriam. He almost sucked me in again."

"Happy to help."

"Well, I've now found the perfect name for Peter Findley. I will no longer call him Peter. From this moment forth, he shall be referred to in all social circles as Peter the Cheater." Miriam and Katie laughed.

Katie went back to the table and instead of calling Peter on his encounter with Abigail and telling him off, she found herself allowing him to continue this charade. It turned out to be an amusing evening as she listened to line after line about how much he loved her.

After they finished their dinner, Katie asked if she could get a desert to take home to Samantha and of course Peter obliged. Katie ordered chocolate layer cake. Then she decided to have a little more fun.

"Peter, I just can't wait to spend this weekend with you."

"Oh, baby, I want to spend it with you too. Unfortunately, I'll be flying to Texas to attend a funeral. An old college buddy of mine passed away."

"That's terrible. I want to show my support in being your devoted girlfriend. I'll go with you."

"No. I insist you stay here. That isn't how I want to start our time together. It just doesn't feel right having you come."

"That's right," Katie thought to herself. "You have plans for Abigail to *come*."

"Listen baby. As soon as I get back, I promise things will get back to normal."

"Right," Katie thought, "That's one normal I want to avoid."

Katie never told Peter about, "the sting," Miriam and she pulled on him. She went home that night and thought about the evening's events. The next morning Katie left Peter a voice mail message stating she had not been totally up front with him. Katie explained she had been seeing someone else since they broke up and in all honesty, she just couldn't betray the other man. Katie told Peter she needed three more months with this other man to be sure of her feelings. She asked him to please not try to contact her since the man spent most of his time at her house.

Several months later, the phone rang. When Katie answered it, she recognized Peter's voice.

"Hi Laura Lee. How's my baby?"

"I don't know Peter, this is Katie. You must have dialed the wrong number."

"Oh! I must have been thinking of you to have dialed your number."

Katie hung up.

That year at Christmas time, Katie was dating a man named Todd who had a beautiful home on the Potomac. Every year Todd had a black-tie Christmas party where he hired people to decorate the house, caterers to fix the food, and a piano player for a medley of Christmas music in the background. Todd sent invitations to his usual guests and told Katie she could invite a girlfriend. Katie had spoken to Miriam, and since Miriam was not dating anyone and had no plans for the evening, she agreed to attend.

To wear at the party, Katie bought a new long silver silk skirt and gray cashmere sweater with crystal buttons adorning the front. The ensemble was way over her budget but she didn't care. She justified it because it was on sale. However, even on sale, it was more than she had ever paid for any one outfit, but it was the classy elegant look she was going for and she told herself she would have numerous opportunities to wear it to different parties.

In the beginning of the evening, Todd and Katie stayed close to the front door, greeting the guests as they entered. Katie could see the waiters carrying silver trays around to all the guests as they served marinated artichokes, stuffed mushrooms, small quiche's, caviar and smoked salmon on crackers. Todd and Katie had been too busy greeting guests to partake in any of the appetizers.

Once the party was in full force they decided to go to the dining room to eat. An elegant buffet table was set with turkey, roast loin, Virginia country ham, new potatoes with parsley, garlic mashed potatoes, fresh green beans and a mixed green salad. On the other side of the room was a desert table displaying apple tarts, chocolate mousse cake, pecan pie and chocolate dipped strawberries.

Todd was stopped at the entrance to the dining room by a group of friends. Katie spotted Miriam and flagged her to join her in the dining room. As they stood there catching up on the evening's events, Katie noticed a familiar face.

"Oh my gosh! Look who just walked in? It's Peter. He's with a date."

"Did you know he was coming?" inquired Miriam.

"No. I never saw the list of people who Todd invited."

Peter immediately walked over to Todd. Just then, Todd waved his hand in a beckoning way, motioning for Katie to come over.

"This ought to be interesting," said Katie. "Are you coming with me?"

"I wouldn't miss it for anything."

As Miriam and Katie walked over to Todd, Peter was busy giving one of the waiters his drink order and didn't notice them until they were standing right in front of him. The second he saw them, the look on his face was one of panic. Katie visualized Peter being tied to the train tracks and wondered if he could hear the train whistle a loud warning of its approach.

Todd gave Katie a kiss, "Katie, I want you to meet a dear friend of mine, Nora Blakley. Her handsome sidekick over here is Peter Findley."

"Nice to meet you," Katie said with a gleam in her eyes.

"Nora and Peter, this is Katie who has so graciously been putting up with me tonight," Todd said as he leaned over and gave Katie another quick kiss. "And this is Katie's friend Miriam."

"So nice to meet you," Nora said as she extended her hand out to both Katie and Miriam.

Peter stood frozen with a phony smile on his face. Katie was sure he saw the headlights of the train.

"Wait. What? Did you say? Miriam? Is her name Miriam?" Peter said as he looked at Todd.

"Yes," replied Todd.

"Better turn up your hearing aid," Nora teased Peter.

It was now dawning on Peter this was not Abigail the aerobics instructor. Peter had heard Katie talk of her friend Miriam, but he had never met her. Had he chosen to attend the parties Katie had invited him to, he would have met Miriam, but alas, he did not.

"So, Nora. How long have you and Peter been dating?" Miriam asked.

"Over eight years now," replied Nora.

"Wow, that's a long time." Turning to Peter, Miriam said, "What was your last name again? Fidelity, I mean Findley?"

Peter looked panicked. "Listen, let's go see where our drinks are?" Peter said excitably to Nora.

"You just gave him the order. Don't be so impatient," said Nora.

"Peter, are you the person I heard about who loves to go to Annapolis to get crabs?" Miriam asked Peter.

"Miriam, don't say crabs!" Katie said laughing. "She means crab cakes, right?"

"Oops! My mistake. You're right," Miriam apologized.

"I don't know what you're talking about. I'm thirsty. I need a drink," exclaimed Peter.

"Go ahead Peter," Nora stated calmly.

"Oh, there's someone I want you to meet. Come on Nora," Peter said as he grabbed Nora by her elbow and pulled her.

"Peter!" Nora objected. "I can walk. I don't have to be pulled."

Choo-choo blew the train whistle. Peter had too many women who had come *all-aboard* his train. It was obvious Peter the Cheater did not want his train to derail.

To this day, Katie still laughs when she thinks of Peter saying, "I only lied because I didn't want to jeopardize what we have with the truth." It goes down in her repertoire of amazing quotes. However, one day Katie heard an even better quote. She was talking with a new friend named Michael. Michael mentioned a friend of his named Peter who was always getting into trouble with women. Katie was amused to find it was the same Peter as Peter the Cheater.

Michael said he knew Peter very well and he could sum Peter up with one quote. As Michael so eloquently put it, "Peter's the type of guy who will always be there, when he needs you."

Conclusion

Dating advice from Colleen Tuohy:

Not all junk mail is bad...sometimes, there are coupons. However, all junk *male* is bad.

If the light bulb is dim, change it.